HE STILL STANDS

Karl Arthur Smink

ISBN: 979-8-9914330-6-8

Dedication

To my sister, whose personal brand of crazy helped inspire Aurelian Vale.

To my friends and colleagues:

To Samantha Z., my editor, whose advice helped me transform this book from something truly strong and moving.

To Elijah, for getting up the nerve to run his very first campaign, which helped birth Daelon and the premise for the story.

To Dart, Derek, Lenny, Nathan, and Ryan for playing in the campaign and deepening the world.

To the people I haven't met, who helped me without knowing:

To Jacob Budz (@xptolevel3), whose infectious humor and love for the game keeps us all going.

To Brennan Lee Mulligan (@BrennanLM), whose masterful storytelling on Dimension 20, as well as his advice on Adventuring Academy, gave me the confidence to run my own game, which has been a resounding success.

To Sam Reich (@samreich), whose charming game shows and personality help me remain confident in being weird and believe that integrity can still exist in the creative industry.

To Antonio Demico (@antodemico) whose cheerful and optimistic experimentation made broaching the subject of homebrew within our game easy and fun.

To Guy Schlanders (@HowToGM) who taught me to notice the reasons for mundane objects in the world, and how they affect the stories told in and around them.

To Red and Blue of Overly Sarcastic Productions (@OSPyoutube), whose Trope Talks and Detail Diatribe series helped me improve my writing and further appreciate the writing of others.

To English Zhongli voice actor Keith Silverstein (@SilverTalkie), whose chilling delivery of the line: "Every journey has its final day; don't rush," helped me breathe over the many, many months of writing, editing, and querying.

To Jed Herne (@Jed_Herne) and Tim Hickson (@TimHickson1), who both gave outstanding writing advice in a digestible format.

Thank you all.

1 - Eating My Words

"Wow, mister," the girl said, staring up at me with her sparkling pink eyes. "I've never seen anyone like you before!"

I smiled, feeling the bandages shift around the edges of my face. From beneath them, a ray of golden light shone out and fell across her. She was a curious sight herself. Pointed ears marked her elven heritage, but the delicate tail swishing behind her spoke of a lineage unfamiliar to me. Lilac-colored skin covered in strange tattoos. She was six. Maybe seven. Bare feet thick with calluses. Her green hair was more knot than braid, and every sharp angle of her body looked like it had been drawn with hunger. Despite this, she seemed incredibly cheerful for a foundling.

She lifted her hand to shield her eyes and turned her head slightly. "What... ARE you?" she asked, squinting through her fingers. "What's your name?"

"I'm called Daelon," I said, pulling the wrapping back over my face. "I am an ethereal; I was written into being by a follower of the old god, Torm."

"Written?" she asked, scrunching her nose. "Like a book?"

"More like a hymn," I said, pointing to the verses written across the wrappings on my chest. "A song too solemn for any chorus. A prayer that learned how to stand."

She pondered this for a moment, then grinned, extending her hand with theatrical flare. "I'm Luna."

I took it, gently. Her fingers were colder than the wind. "It's a pleasure to meet you, Luna."

The wagon jostled, iron-rung wheels complaining against the path's neglect. We rode in a cart meant for cargo, not passengers—sacks of grain were our seats, and the air smelled of burlap and old dust. Yet she scooted closer, practically buzzing.

"Do you glow all the time? Can you fly?"

"Some days the light shines dimmer than others, but it is always there." I chuckled. "And I walk, like you."

"Grub's up!" the carriage driver bellowed from the front. Luna sprang up, giddily clapping as a rough arm shoved its way through the curtain, clutching a half round of dark horsebread. She seized it with both hands like it was a royal feast.

The bread was dry, cracking as she broke it in two. She held out the larger piece towards me.

"That's your share!" she said brightly.

She looked so certain. So proud, even. Like she'd done something good. Like sharing meant she was real, and kind, and not as forgotten as the world kept trying to tell her she was.

I hesitated. I didn't need it.

I hadn't needed food since the day I was written. Not the warmth of fire, nor the breath of air, nor the sleep of night. I existed outside those wants. But I remembered what it meant to eat.

I remembered the hush that falls between bites, the way two people sitting side by side can feel less alone when their hunger is mutual. I remembered that food wasn't always about sustenance. Sometimes, it was about ceremony. About kindness. About not having to hide.

And I knew—without needing to ask—that she rarely got to share a meal without first stealing it. That she probably had to chew in alley shadows, arms around her knees, guarding every swallow like it might be the last.

This moment was sacred to her. Not the bread, but the *sharing* of it. To correct her would be cruel. To refuse her gift would be worse.

So I took it.

"Thank you," I said gently, bowing my head as I accepted the offering. The weight of it was light in my hand, but the gesture was heavy. She didn't have enough. That much was obvious just by looking at her.

Her legs were no thicker than my wrist. Her cheeks, though wide from her smile, were sunken. Yet her eyes—those unreasonably pink, too-bright eyes—were alive with joy. As if the world hadn't been cruel to her, or perhaps, she simply hadn't learned to see it that way yet.

She tore into her half like it was sweetcake.

"Mmm!" she mumbled through a mouthful. "It's so good, right?"

I looked at the crumbling edge of mine, at the pale mold beginning to grey just beneath the crust. At least three days old. Maybe four. The flour was coarsely milled. I imagined it would have taken real effort to swallow—if I were the sort who needed to. It was the kind of bread no merchant would sell unless desperate.

I didn't say any of that.

"It's wonderful," I told her instead. And I ate. Not out of need, but out of mercy. Out of guilt. Out of reverence.

She beamed. A child with nothing to give, giving everything to a stranger she met not two hours ago. The driver had warned me about her when I climbed aboard: said they'd found her sitting under a tree at Duskmire, alone. She was lost and looking for her parents. The driver and his wife said they'd rather bring her someplace safe than leave her to the wilds, since they were headed to the capital anyway. They offered me the same courtesy. They hadn't asked for coin, just said there was space in the back and that I looked like I had been walking for 'quite a spell'. They were certainly right about that.

Luna's legs dangled off the cart edge, too short to touch earth, and swung in rhythm with the rattle of wheels. There was a peace to it, in that moment. I'd almost forgotten what it meant to feel safe enough to eat next to someone.

She leaned against me, cheek brushing fabric.

And I let her.

Because whatever else I was, I could at least be *that.* A wall to lean on. A place where, even just for tonight, she didn't have to be strong.

The sun dipped lower, casting the world in red-gold light, and for a moment, I could almost pretend. Pretend that I could still bring comfort to someone who desperately needed it.

2 - Burdens of the Past

Night fell slowly. It folded like a drape pulled gently over the sky, too slow to startle, too complete to ignore. The wagon creaked in softer rhythm now. The reins had changed hands; I could hear it in the hum, someone new guiding the beast. Whoever it was, they sang to the darkness like it might sing back.

Luna slept beside me, knees tucked tight to her chest, her tail looped around her ankles. Every breath she took felt borrowed, uneven, as if some part of her didn't trust the air.

I watched her. Not like a guard. Like a witness.

She was inked from jaw to heel. What I'd taken for dye in daylight now glimmered faintly, pulsing every so often with that too-familiar sheen of arcane magic. It wasn't fear that sat heavy in my chest, it was a question. I hated that I already suspected the answer.

I pulled back the cloth over my palm, just enough for a sliver of light to spill out. I angled it toward her shoulder, letting it catch the edge of the ink, searching for details in the designs.

These weren't marks of heritage. They were runes. Bindings. Someone had tried to lock something in. I'd seen patterns like these before. But never so many. Never on someone so small.

She stirred.

Her face scrunched, half-aware, and she lifted one arm to shield her eyes. Her lashes fluttered open, unfocused at first, then narrowed. The glow reflected back at me in that dull pink.

I covered the light immediately, tucking the wrapping back in place with practiced ease. My hands were still.

"You glow," she mumbled, the words catching on the fray of her yawn.

"I'm sorry," I whispered.

She didn't recoil. But she didn't smile, either.

Instead, she rubbed her eyes and let out a long, slow breath, like exhaling something she didn't have the words for. "You were looking at my tattoos."

"I was."

"They hurt a lot," she said quietly. Then, after a pause: "Do you remember who gave you yours?"

I looked down at the scripture spiraling across my arms, the verses that shaped me, held me. Prayers I had not written, in a language most had long forgotten. Mine were not chains like hers. But still... they were not freely chosen.

"No," I said softly. "Only that someone believed they mattered."

She didn't answer.

Sleep had taken her again, dragging her back beneath her curious consciousness. I stayed where I was, unmoving, the glow sealed beneath cloth, the questions behind teeth.

And I listened. I knew now why each breath came shallow. The pain of the tattoos etched tremors into her rest, enough to thin her breaths into careful measures. She slept beside me.

How? With skin raw from ink, with bones sharp from hunger, with a body barely holding together? And still she slept.

And I sat in the dark, ashamed of every comfort I did not need.

A few hours before dawn, the wagon rolled to a gentle halt at the edge of the hamlet. The road, if it could still be called that, was little more than well-worn earth, tamped smooth by years of quiet coming and going. Modest homes slouched in irregular clusters on either side. Only one chimney smoked. The rest slumbered under sagging roofs and shuttered windows.

"Boeth," the driver grunted, stretching his neck with a crack. "Last stop before Rarek. We'll head out again when the sun's up proper. 'Til then, rest while you can. Town's quiet. Safe enough."

Luna didn't move. I eased myself off the back of the wagon, landing softly, and began to walk, letting the hush of the road swallow the sound of my steps. When I had put enough distance between us, I reached up and loosened the band around my hand. The wrappings slipped free in silence, and golden light flowed out like water from a cracked vessel.

Boeth was a whisper of a village. No more than a dozen buildings, most tilting with age. An overturned wheelbarrow slept beside a long-shuttered shop. Ivy blanketed the walls of a nearby shed, as if the forest had begun to reclaim what the people no longer could.

Half-hidden between two crooked homes, a chapel stood with its steeple barely breaching the roofline. The structure leaned, slightly off-center, but it had not fallen. Even here, in this place too small for politics, where relics survived by being overlooked, the chapel stood sealed. Its doors boarded. No offerings. No candlelight behind the panes. And there, etched into stone worn soft by years and rain, was a symbol I hadn't beheld in an age.

One of Torm's lineage. A sibling deity, born of the same forgotten pantheon. One of the quiet ones. The ones no one slandered because no one remembered. The carving had faded, its lines dulled by moss and time, but the shape endured: an open hand, encircled by thorns woven into a laurel. Mercy bound to resolve.

I let the glow from my palm intensify, enough to trace the emblem clearly, enough to feel sure. Something in my posture eased without asking. A relic still standing, not because anyone demanded it, but because it hadn't yet fallen to the cruel decay of time.

I brightened more.

More light than I needed. More than the night called for. I let it spill over the stone like sun over frost, hoping it might feel the warmth. Hoping it would remember what it meant to be seen.

The carving caught the glow unevenly—its grooves softened by age, its edges lost to weather and neglect—but for a moment, it looked whole. Almost new.

No offerings adorned the sill. No incense marked the air. The boards across the door had warped from rain and years. Yet the symbol remained. Forgotten; no one had bothered to destroy it.

It was a quiet kind of reverence, standing there. Letting the light reach what time had dimmed. And though the emblem didn't move, didn't speak, something about the way it held the light made my chest ache. Like I was looking at a grave that still waited for its mourner.

I stayed longer than I meant to, letting the silence press close, letting it settle in the hollow space just beneath my ribs. The symbol above did not accuse nor beckon. It simply endured.

Most eyes—human, divine, or otherwise—search, want, command.

This one remembered.

As if some silent part of me had stirred at the sight, I murmured, "I remember, too." And standing beneath it, I didn't feel quite so forgotten.

A scuff of boots over loose stone pulled my gaze from the chapel. I turned just as the torchlight crested the hill behind me.

The man who approached wasn't armored. He looked like a farmer drafted into the role of watchman. Tired eyes, lined more by weather than age, blinked stiffly. His rough-cut vest lay over a linen shirt, frayed rope cinched his trousers, and a cudgel swung lazily at his hip.

He raised the torch higher, trying to see me better.

"Out for a walk, are you?" he asked, voice neutral.

"Couldn't sleep," I lied. I lifted my right arm, palm open toward him. A sign of peace. Of humility. Of hands unarmed and pockets clean.

The man flinched, twisting away with a grimace as my light struck him full in the face. He lifted an arm to shield his eyes, and I winced at the oversight, already reaching up to bind the glow in cloth once more.

"Stars above," he muttered, rubbing one eye with the heel of his hand. He blinked hard, torch tilting in his grip. When he looked at me again, it was slower—studying. His gaze paused on the wrapped layers across my face, my hands. The soft gold leaking from the seams.

"You one o' them glow-folk?" he asked.

I offered the faintest smile. "Ethereal. Yes."

He grunted, scratching at the back of his neck, the torch bobbing slightly with the motion. "Heard stories. Didn't reckon any of you were still… y'know." He circled a finger vaguely near his temple, then let the gesture falter into an awkward half-wave. "Thought you'd all gone mad."

I didn't flinch. That rumor had teeth. Some of which I'd pulled myself. I'd seen the light go out in more than one ethereal, seen the duty that once shimmered beneath their wrappings fade to dead ash. When their light vanished, or changed color, what remained was something empty. Their bodies walked, spoke sometimes. But there was no purpose in them. No weight to their words, no tether to who they'd been. One of them—I won't name her—had to be stopped before she convinced others to abandon their verses as well.

"Some lose their light. Forget who they are. What they were made for. Go… hollow." My eyes drifted to the chapel behind him. "But not all of us."

He followed my gaze, turning slowly toward the chapel. A low whistle escaped through his teeth.

"Don't reckon anyone's spared a glance for that place in years," he said. "Used to be candles in the windows. A hymnal nailed to the door. Now it's birds nesting in the eaves and dust thick enough to leave a handprint."

"Still," I said, "it stands."

He nodded, lips pursing. "Aye. Don't rightly know why. Doubt anyone remembers whose god it was."

"I do," I said softly. The words weren't meant for him.

He didn't ask. Just dipped his chin once, like he understood what not to say.

I didn't explain. What good would it do? The old gods still had their names etched into stone, but not into hearts. The world had outgrown sacrifice. It didn't want gods who asked for virtue or restraint.

I wasn't going to fault a farmer for forgetting. But I felt the absence of Torm throbbing louder in places like this: half-remembered shrines to a pantheon the world had let decay.

"You bound for Rarek?" he asked after a moment.

"I am."

He gave a small nod, like that made sense. Rarek still carried the name, after all. The last city to hold on, if only in symbol. Decades ago, the chapel had been full, the scripture recited with the weight it deserved. Now, it was all costumes and pageantry—faith turned into fashion. Those who still *believed* had become something of an oddity. And those like me, who lived by the code, we were something worse. A mirror the people didn't want held up to them.

He frowned, thumb skimming the edge of his torch's handle. "Heard things've gotten worse out that way. More talk about your kind. About Torm. Some folks saying it's not safe to be… well. *Seen.*"

I met his eyes with a tired smile. "That song's always been playing. The volume just changes."

He gave a thoughtful grunt. "S'pose that's true."

As if to contrast the roaring songs of the capital, the silence of the night flowed in to take the place of our words. Even the night was listening.

Then he nodded again. "Just keep your light dim when you hit the gates, yeah? No sense in welcomin' trouble."

"Thank you," I said.

He gave a small grunt, then raised his torch in a rough sort of farewell before turning away. His footsteps faded quickly, eventually swallowed by the stillness.

I lingered a moment longer, facing the chapel.

The steeple sagged, the doors were barred, the windows little more than splinters clinging to their frames. But the mark still held. Weathered, yes. Faded, forgotten, ignored... but still there. Mercy and resolve.

Maybe that was all faith ever really was. Not fire from the heavens or voices in the storm. Just… memory. Etched into stone. Carried forward by the few who refused to let it vanish.

I turned, and began the walk back to the wagon.

Rarek would not be kind.

It hadn't been for some time. The city had grown louder, harder, more cynical in the years since I first arrived. What reverence remained had become currency—sold in pieces by those who no longer believed, but knew how to profit from those who still pretended to. Tailors and trinket-sellers hawked Tormite pins and engraved brooches in market stalls, peddling righteousness like jewelry, while the chapel's pews sat empty.

Rarek was the last place on the map where Torm's name still held even a sliver of cultural weight. Outside the capital, the faith had all but vanished, left behind like a tattered flag. People had seen through the pantomime. They'd stopped looking to the heavens and started looking at each other, each asking the same thing: *'What's in it for me?'*

My sisters and I had remained because we remembered a time before that question became a creed. Because someone had to. For all its rot and mockery, Rarek was still ours. The chapel still stood, which meant our vow to the city still held.

I wasn't welcome in Rarek. Not really. Not by the ones who mattered. Every time I returned, the air felt a little thinner, the stares a little longer, the silence after I passed just a little too practiced.

But the trail had ended, again. The roads had run out. So I would go back. Rest. Wait. Search anew.

I wasn't returning for comfort. Or for kindness. I was returning because something still called to me there: something unfinished, unanswered. If I could find the hand that made me, perhaps I could find the shape of the faith again. Not just for myself, but for what remained of Rarek.

The chapel's silhouette lingered in my periphery as I made my way back toward the wagon. The owners were still asleep. The lantern by the driver's bench had burned out. The horses stood still, ears twitching at ghosts only they could hear. I stepped carefully across the gravel, preparing to return to my spot beside Luna—

She wasn't there.

Something inside me clenched. She was so small. Fragile. The woods here were old, thick with undergrowth and moonless dark. Even without beasts, there were worse things in the world than teeth and claws.

I turned slowly, scanning the square. My light flared a little brighter, just in case. I was preparing to call her name, with every muscle coiled to run. Something shifted near the inn's side wall. A flicker of motion, barely more than a shadow unpeeling itself from another. I turned to face it.

And there she was.

Luna shuffled into view, wiping her mouth lazily on the back of her arm, her feet dragging in that pliant, half-sleep way children move when their bodies haven't quite agreed to wakefulness. Her eyes carried a faint glow now, a muted pink pulse that came and went like breath on glass. She was awake, or close enough to pass for it.

The tightness in my chest eased with a slow, silent exhale. Had I been *breathing?*

"Where did you go?" I asked, stepping toward her.

She blinked at me, groggy and unamused. "Water," she said, as if it was obvious. "The horses have a bucket."

I winced, a sour taste curdling in my mouth as I spoke. "The *trough*?"

"Yeah." She shuffled past me, climbing up into the wagon. She sat down and squinted back at me through a tangle of green hair. "Why are you staring?"

"I was worried," I said, honestly. "You were gone."

"I was thirsty." She yawned, long and unbothered, and curled back up like a cat. The glow in her eyes flickered once, then held steady, dimming gently as she drifted. Sleep reclaiming her like it had only paused. It was as if her body had learned to seize rest the moment it was allowed, trained by necessity to steal sleep wherever it could be safely taken.

I remained standing, watching her for a moment longer. So much defiance wrapped in such a fragile frame.

So little explanation for the burden she carried. And yet there she was. Parched, half-asleep, and drinking from a horse trough without complaint.

I eased down beside her again, slow and quiet. She didn't stir. Above us, the stars had begun to retreat behind a veil of grey. Dawn would find us soon. And Rarek, not long after.

After the sun breached the hills, we loaded the wagon in silence. Morning clung to everything. Dew steamed from the canvas, cold air caught in the joints of tired wood. The wheels groaned awake, slow and reluctant, as we turned east. The driver muttered something about reaching the capital by noon if the horses didn't lose heart.

Luna settled cross-legged beside me, quieter than before. The spark hadn't vanished, but it had drawn inward—folded down into something smaller, tighter. The constant questions, the unfiltered joy… all focused now, like a silent painter.

She held two rough burlap figures in her lap, their twine limbs bent from use. The kind of makeshift dolls you'd expect to see discarded behind a weaver's shop. One wore a faded strip of red ribbon. The other had a dark stain down its side: berry, I thought. She bounced them playfully in her hands, not speaking.

I'd seen a thousand faces from a hundred corners of the world. Rarek itself was a mosaic of castes, clans, and tongues. But the child before me didn't match any of them. Her features were soft and elven, but not quite like the forest-born who still came down from the northern ridge. And those bindings—I'd only ever seen them made by guild leaders, burned into the skin of apostate mages before they were turned out of a major city.

Curiosity, more than anything, held my gaze. I waited a beat, then asked gently, "Where are you from, Luna?"

She didn't look up, still focused on angling one of the dolls so it could perch atop a loop of coiled rope like a watchman. "Silverstrand Enclave," she said plainly.

I frowned. "Doesn't sound familiar. Where is that?"

With a shrug so casual it could've been habit, she said "Somewhere else. Past the veil."

"The veil?" I echoed, keeping my voice light. "What does that mean?"

"It's where the real sky is," she said, like it was obvious. "Where the waterfalls go sideways, and the sun remembers your name. Everything's soft there. Except the flowers. They bite."

I studied her face, searching for the gap between story and truth. She wasn't smiling.

"With your family?" I asked.

She nodded, raising the red-ribboned doll and letting it perform a clumsy dive off the crate's edge. "My mom, my dad, my sister. And me, when I was little."

My head tilted. *When she was little.* She couldn't have weighed more than a sack of grain. She had limbs like broom handles and slept like she was used to waking to danger.

"Little?" I asked, more gently than skeptically.

She didn't answer. Just caught the falling doll, reset it on the rope like nothing had happened, and kept the events going between them—softer now, fragmented. Her hands had lost their bouncy playfulness, like they no longer belonged to the game.

"You don't live there anymore?" I asked.

The dolls slipped from her hands. They fell into the straw with the quietest rustle and didn't rise again. She didn't reach for them. Her back was to me, shoulders small and rigid, drawn in so tightly she might've disappeared if I blinked.

I shifted forward. "Luna?"

A breath answered me—wet and uneven. The tremble of something raw pressing up against the edge of her restraint. The sound of a child trying to be quiet, because loudness hadn't helped her before.

By the right hand of Tyr… what did I say?

I reached out, slow and deliberate, letting my hand settle on her shoulder like one might test the strength of cracked glass. When I turned her toward me, her lip trembled. Her eyes, glassy and overfull, shone with the weight of something she hadn't learned how to name. Her breath hitched again, ragged but deathly silent. What kind of life teaches a child to cry like that?

I opened one arm to her, leaving space. In case she needed somewhere safe to fall. Then I moved my other hand from her shoulder to the back of her head, brushing it once with quiet reassurance.

She recoiled—so fast and so violently it barely registered as human. Her limbs twisted like a burning spider, and in the span of a breath, she'd wrenched backward, slipping clean through the small of my arm. She struck the side wall of the wagon hard enough to rattle the frame.

I didn't move. The glow beneath the wrappings on my arms was steady and strong, but completely covered. How had she phased through me?

Her eyes met mine—wide, unblinking, burning. The glow behind them pulsed brighter than before. Red. Startling. Wrong.

"Everything alright back there?" the driver called over his shoulder.

Her eyes flicked toward the sound, and something shifted. The tension bled from her frame all at once, like a string cut at both ends. She blinked, slowly, and the glow dulled—back to that soft pink. The tears she'd been holding finally slipped free, carving quiet paths down her cheeks. She didn't speak. Just curled in on herself, knees drawn tight, head pressed into the corner like she was trying to vanish into the wood.

I lowered my arms and leaned back, careful not to let the boards creak beneath me. The weight in the space between us was suffocating.

"Yes," I called, the word catching in my throat. "Just… a misunderstanding."

She didn't turn.

And I didn't move.

Not five paces apart, and I couldn't have reached her if I tried.

Something had broken this girl, bent her into a shape that flinched from care. I didn't know what. Didn't know who. Her parents? Her sister? Were they gone—or worse, the cause?

But she wasn't in any place to explain. And I wasn't about to make her try.

3 - Remembrance, the Day of Miracles

Luna stayed curled tight in her corner, quiet and unmoving, though the stiffness in her shoulders had softened little by little. Sleep didn't find her. Not really. Just that half-waking stillness children learn when they've had to hide too often. I'd seen it before. Caused it, more than once. My presence might've been just another thing she didn't trust the dark to protect her from.

I didn't look at her directly. Didn't speak. My mind churned with questions I didn't know how to voice. Or when it might be safe to try. Every word felt too loud before it was ever spoken.

She looked impossibly small from across the wagon bed. Looked farther away than she'd been even when missing.

Hours passed, stretched thin and brittle. The silence between us held like glass—fragile, full of pressure, always on the edge of shatter. Then the driver's voice cut through the hush like a stone skipping over still water. "Rarek, dead ahead."

Luna stirred at the sound, her pointed ears flickering with motion that seemed to break the spell. She didn't speak. Just glanced toward me—quick and sidelong, like a bird checking the distance between itself and a predator. Measuring.

Then she crawled forward on quiet hands and knees, slipped past the crates, and pulled open the front flaps.

Sunlight flooded in as Luna parted the canvas, striking sharp against the gloom of the wagon. Beyond her shoulder, the high outer walls of Rarek rose into view.

From the road, Rarek looked as it always had: a bulwark against the wild. A city built to repel, that never once refused entry. A stronghold untouched by siege, slowly corroded by apathy, not war. Its surfaces were clean, impeccably maintained, weathered only by wind and rain. Its function had become theater.

But this was Rarek. Still home, I supposed.

There were things I looked forward to. A library with more volumes than dust. Benches not yet overtaken by vines. My sisters, strange and steady in their own ways, who somehow still endured here too.

But coming back without answers… again… tasted like failure. I could sense the city had changed, as it often did during my absences. And I could feel, as always, that it expected I had changed with it. I hadn't. I didn't think I could.

Beneath the groan of wheels and the tired clop of hooves, a cacophony of brass and tin clanged out from within the distant city. Each bell tolling a slightly different tune, like a choir without a conductor. Festive. Unrestrained.

Remembrance.

Once, the Day of Miracles had been sacred. A quiet time marked by reflection and vows renewed, peace over pride, sacrifice over spectacle. A covenant, remembered.

Now it was noise. Markets spilling into the streets. Painted faces and hollow rituals. Dancers with wings stitched from silk and string, performing a story no one knew the words to anymore. They bought their reverence in booths, wrapped it in colored cloth, and tossed the old meanings away like husks. Banners rippled atop the weary walls, their colors bold and brash, parading themselves like they held meaning that hadn't long since thinned into decoration.

Luna's ears perked, twitching in time with the chiming bells, and a soft gasp slipped from her lips as something clicked behind her eyes. Recognition bloomed across her face—joyful, sudden, and unburdened. In an instant, it was as if the weight of the morning had never touched her. I caught the observation as soon as it sparked, and tucked it away. I wasn't about to ruin the first good moment she'd had since the incident.

The wagon creaked to a halt. Before the wheels had fully settled, she was already on the move, scrambling toward the back with that wild energy I hadn't seen since yesterday. I reached out on instinct, then caught myself.

"How do you know about Remembrance?" I asked.

She twisted around mid-crawl, beaming. "I was here for it last year!"

I stared after her, the smile still etched on her face as she ducked through the canvas flap. Last year. That would've made her... five. Out on the streets of Rarek at five years old. Wandering, alone.

I slipped my satchel over my shoulder. Far too light, considering the months and miles I'd burned, and the nothing I'd returned with. But as I glanced down at the eager girl impatiently waiting to speed off into the crowd, my bitterness melted away. I stepped down beside her.

"I know a singer here," I said, a smile tugging at the edge of my voice. "The best in the city. Want to meet her?"

Her mouth fell open in an exaggerated, breathless gape. "Do I *ever*!"

I turned to the driver and pressed a few coins into his hand.

"Always glad to help someone reclaim a few steps," he said, adjusting his hat with a weathered thumb. He gave a small, knowing nod. "Especially the ones who've spent too many going forward." Then he tipped his chin past me. "That one's not slowing down. You'd better move."

I turned. Luna was already gone, a flash of green darting into the festival crowd like a ribbon caught in wind.

I hurried after her, eyes locked on the streak of tangled hair threading its way between carts and clumps of revelers. She was fast—faster than she had any right to be. She never broke stride, even when the path ahead closed tight. She slipped through bodies and carts with uncanny ease, vanishing behind crates only to reappear yards ahead, never so much as brushing a shoulder.

More than once, I lost her entirely. No gap wide enough for passage, no pause to explain how she'd made it through. I nearly collided with a pair of dwarves rounding a stall. They cursed; I apologized, and pressed on. Wherever she was headed, she wasn't waiting.

Every few strides, she stopped to marvel at something. A cart of lacquered masks, a rack of candied fruit, a merchant's table exploding with dyed fabrics. She twirled into a circle of dancing children as though she'd always been one of them, laughing like it had never been any other way.

Her joy was magnetic. A few nearby vendors tensed, watching her small, darting form like they expected a theft. But once it was clear she meant no harm, only to greet them, to smile, they eased. The older women grinned, politely waving her along. Luna twirled near a knot of children, her feet keeping a rhythm the musicians barely managed. Their laughter rose above the bells and clatter, shining through Rarek's usual foggy haze like long-lost sunlight.

But it was me she pulled toward her with every wide-eyed glance and delighted shout. For a moment, the city didn't feel so heavy.

The streets pulsed with variety. Lizardfolk arguing prices with halflings perched on stacked crates. Orcs straining to help a gnome string lanterns across a crooked bakery roof. Dozens of elves from half as many bloodlines gliding through the crowd in silks, ribbons, or hardened leather.

Yet none of them looked like her. Even here in Rarek, where scales, fur, horns, and tusks brushed shoulders without comment, she was still different. Lilac skin. A cowlike tail with too fine a motion for any beastfolk lineage I knew. And those eyes—glistening like kunzite saucers as they took in every color and shape in the reveling city.

I searched my memory again, scouring every tale and map and record I'd come across for any mention of a Silverstrand Enclave. A place with sideways waterfalls and biting flowers. A real sky.

Nothing.

I looked up. The skyline was familiar, even beneath the banners and garlands draped from wall to wall. Crimson and gold flared in the wind, dancing over rooftops like they'd always belonged there. Vendors bellowed their wares—sugar-glazed roots, scented oils, garish festival hats tall enough to need balancing straps. Flags flapped from railings and chimneys. And from nearly every window and doorframe, bells rang out in uneven harmony, each a note in the city's ragged chorus.

This was Remembrance in name only. It used to be a time of reflection, of silence shared between neighbors. The people remembered when there wasn't enough. When candles were rationed, and meals meant choosing who ate well and who didn't eat at all. The old rites didn't glorify hunger, but they honored the act of going without. They asked us to remember how we endured it, together. Sacrifice wasn't pain for pain's sake, it was a promise. A belief that tomorrow would be built by what we willingly gave up today.

Now, the festivals screamed abundance. Tables sagged with food no one finished. Merchandise used for less than a day before it was discarded. A city pretending the lean years were over just because there was enough to waste.

That was the trick, though. You make something bright enough, and no one looks at the shadows. These fireworks, parades, and feasts weren't celebration. They were misdirection. A city built on scarcity distracting itself with flash and noise, so it didn't have to accept how little it truly had. A deficit of tradition, purpose, and memory.

Now it was color. Motion. Volume.

...and joy.

I couldn't deny that. People were smiling. Rarek didn't get much of that anymore. A bit of lightness was overdue, even if it came wrapped in gaudy cloth and stripped of meaning. I only wished it hadn't cost so much of what the day had stood for.

For a holiday devoted to memory, it was remarkable how much it seemed to forget.

As if to dispel my rumination, a requious sound reached me. Soft at first, like a thread pulled through a tapestry, winding its way between handbells, hawkers, and clattering boots. A voice, mournful yet strong, rising in minor intervals like a prayer remembered halfway through mourning.

Kirtana.

Luna heard it too. Her ears flicked, her posture shifted. She didn't speak—just peeled away from the cluster of children and walked toward the sound, as if summoned. I followed, letting the requiem draw us both like tide to shore.

Every note loosened something in me, just enough to make the weight bearable. It was the kind of sound that made space. Space to breathe. Space to feel.

We turned a corner and found her.

Kirtana stood tall in the square's alcove. Her face was unwrapped—blinding, bare, unashamed. The loose ends of her bandages stirred in the wind like strands of sunlit hair.

Barely two dozen people stood around her, rapt. A quiet congregation amid the chaos. Her light cast a halo over the small crowd that pressed back the morning's harshness.

Even Luna stilled. No bounce, no twirl, no fidget. Just wide eyes, caught in the glow, reflecting the radiance that flowed so freely from Kirtana.

When the final note faded, no one spoke. A few clapped—quiet, reverent—but most just stood, suspended in the hush she left behind. Some wept. Others bowed their heads. No one wanted to be the first to move.

Kirtana reached up to rewrap her face. The light dimmed, allowing space for the sunlight to fill in the void it left behind. The crowd shifted, and Luna managed to dart through. I lifted a hand, thinking to stop her, but there was no catching her curiosity. She appeared at Kirtana's side in a blink, unleashing a barrage of questions too fast to separate.

Kirtana paused, one last strip of linen still loose in her hand, and turned to her unexpected guest. Her smile was patient. Unhurried. She listened—truly listened—then knelt, tying the final wrap with care before speaking to the child in a voice so quiet it stilled Luna without resistance.

I made my way through the thinning ring of onlookers. She saw me before I spoke, and her smile shifted—gentle, knowing.

"Well, well," she said, her voice still carrying that sacred tone. "It seems you've found your way home, brother."

Luna spun toward me, face plastered with disbelief. "She's your *sister?*"

I nodded, the smile forming before I could stop it. "I told you I knew the best singer in Rarek."

Kirtana stood, smoothing the front of her wrappings, and gave me a look more exasperated than stern. "Daelon," she sighed, the tone not scolding so much as reminding, "*Let no tongue dress itself in praise that hasn't first tasted silence.*"

I tilted my head slightly, letting a sliver of light slip through the folds. "If I'm not allowed to praise you, sister, then who is? We might be stitched from the same cloth, but we're not the same thread. I've never quieted a square with a single breath." I nodded toward the small crowd still hovering at the edge of where her voice had touched them—unwilling to break the spell. "I can't sing. That's why *you're* The Song of Heaven."

Kirtana gave the faintest huff of laughter, the kind that barely lifted the cloth around her face. "I haven't forgotten the meaning of my own name," she murmured, a flicker of dry amusement in her tone.

"That's so pretty!" Luna chimed in. She darted to my side and tugged gently at my sleeve, her fingers all knuckle and bone. "What does *your* name mean?"

I paused. The glow inside me dimmed, subtle but felt. "Daelon Caelux," I said. "It means… Messenger of Heaven."

Luna cocked her head. "What's your message?"

The question struck harder than I expected. Words caught like gravel in my chest. I looked away.

Before the silence could tighten, Kirtana knelt and touched Luna's shoulder with two careful fingers.

"When the time is right," she said, "I'm sure he'll tell us."

Luna glanced down at Kirtana's hand on her shoulder—wrapped, gentle, still aglow in places. She didn't flinch. Just blinked slowly, nodded once with a small "Okay," and slipped away. Her slight frame vanished into the press of color and sound like a fish sliding back into the current.

I took a step to follow.

"Let her go, Daelon."

Kirtana's voice was soft, but anchored. Enough to stop me mid-stride.

I turned to protest, half-formed words catching against the ache in my chest. "She's hurt. She's lost. She's hungry and—"

"She moves like a spirited fawn. She weaves through a crowd like she was born to it, and this is the one day no stomach in Rarek goes unfed," she said evenly. "Whatever's been done to her… it didn't break her, and it won't today."

"Kirtana, you didn't see—"

"I saw what you saw," she said, cutting gently. "An orphaned fae child. Bound to something we don't understand. More potent magic swirling behind her eyes than guild-trained sorcerers. A child carrying things no child should have to." I'd seen that look of pity and understanding on her face before. It was the one she gave me whenever I was in too deep. The one she wore right before saying something I knew was right, and simply couldn't accept. "But she's not your charge, Daelon."

I looked away, toward the crowd, where the sound of handbells had swallowed the last place I'd seen her.

"She'll be fine," Kirtana said, knowing my face without seeing it.

And perhaps she would be. Perhaps she already was. But the feeling gnawed anyway. Low, persistent, rooted too deep for reason to reach. Kirtana wasn't wrong. Luna didn't need help.

But she did.

And I didn't know how to carry both truths in the same hand.

Kirtana was quiet for a long moment. When she finally spoke, it was softer than before. "You can care for someone, brother… without trying to carry all their weight. If you wish to offer your aid to someone who needs it, come with me."

I followed Kirtana through the courtyard and into the chapel beyond, a modest structure that carried the hush of long-held reverence. Inside its walls, Rarek didn't protect its people anymore—it protected its performance. The chapel was the only structure still honest. A whisper of faith buried beneath the pageantry of a city desperate to forget what it once revered.

It looked as though it might collapse under a heavy breeze, but someone had loved it well, tended it like an ailing elder who still had stories to tell. The pews creaked with memory, their old wood splintered in places, but wiped clean. The threadbare carpet bore no pattern I could name, only the even marks of recent sweeping; the tracks of someone too kind to let dust win. I followed an arc of light as it filtered through fractured panes of stained glass, casting scattered reds, greens, and purples along the walls. It was still beautiful. Just… quiet in its beauty. Like a face you'd loved once that had since forgotten how to smile.

Kirtana moved ahead without sound, gliding between rows with a solemn grace. Her fingers hovered above the empty pews, not touching, but close enough to acknowledge them. At the front, the shrine stood clean and gleaming, its edges dulled by years of touch from faithful hands. Before it, two humans knelt in prayer. They were the only other souls here, a testament to the inversion of Remembrance roaring outside in the streets. This day used to bring out worshipers in droves, pews spilling into the isles as people stood and bowed their heads together.

The space beside the kneeling figures, where the shrine's guardian usually stood watch like a blade planted in the earth, was empty.

"Where is Eryndra?" I asked quietly.

Kirtana didn't turn. Her voice came light and distant, joining the dust still drifting in the morning light. "Civil unrest's been growing worse. Without Torm's light to guide them, the people are becoming focused on their personal needs, and many of them are displeased. The city needs bodies in uniform. The guard knows as well as any of us that the shrine here doesn't exactly need someone posted here full time. Not with fewer than ten visitors a week." She paused, then added, "Our sister has been called to... *quell* that unrest more and more since your last visit. Even before the festival riled everyone up."

The word 'visit' hung in the air like an accusation.

I'd spent the better part of the last two years anywhere but Rarek. Chasing shadows. Following every whisper that might lead me to the one who'd written me into being. Meanwhile, the congregation here had continued to wither. And though it wasn't fair, part of me resented the implication. What did she expect? That I abandon my search? That I stay and preach sermons to empty pews? If anyone could convince people of the truth and beauty of Torm, it was Kirtana. But without me here to temper her, I could only imagine how Eryndra's intensity had swelled to fill the vacuum. There were gentler hands than hers to nourish a wavering flock; tact wasn't exactly her specialty.

Kirtana drifted to the shrine and placed a wrapped hand on the shoulder of the old woman kneeling there. Selva stirred slowly, blinking out of her reverence, her eyes adjusting to the soft gold leaking from Kirtana's light. A tired but genuine smile curved her lips. "Nice to have a quiet Remembrance, for once," Selva rasped, her voice like the rustle of dried leaves.

"A blessed hush," I replied as I stepped closer, the words falling from my mouth on instinct. An old Tormite phrase, nearly extinct.

Selva's eyes turned to me, warm with recognition.

"Do you know where Eryndra was called to today?" I asked her.

Selva nodded with a weary kind of knowing, then sighed. "Something about revelers tearing up the fountain again."

Of course. If there was unrest in the square and Eryndra was within earshot, peace wouldn't be long behind. But she had a way of enforcing calm with a clenched fist, and bruises were the best the offenders could hope for. To Eryndra, stillness by force was still stillness.

"I'd better go see if I can find her," I said, already turning to go.

Kirtana's hand found my shoulder—firm, light with pressure but heavy with intention. She didn't have to speak for me to feel the shape of the question. She asked anyway. "I take it, by your reaction to the fae child's question... that your search was unsuccessful?"

I said nothing. I didn't need to. She'd heard the pause. Seen the weight it left behind. Sometimes silence said it clearer than grief.

"Luna," I said finally.

"Pardon?"

"Her name is Luna." I stepped out from under her touch. It wasn't unkind, but I couldn't bear its warmth—how easily it folded into quiet disapproval.

Without looking back, I made my way down the aisle and pushed into the noise of the city once more. The garish light, the bells, the sugar-slick air. This holy-day-turned-harvest-festival. A facade of joyful opulence that would vanish as soon as the sun went down. I let it swallow me whole.

I pushed through the garlands and merchant carts, the swell of faces pressing around me, making my way towards the fountain. But something broke my focus. A voice, rich and delivered with steady assurance, the kind that didn't just rise above a crowd, but carried through it. Not shouting... not singing...

Preaching.

My steps slowed. Even on the Remembrances of old, the gods were rarely invoked aloud. A private prayer, a half-whispered hymn, but public sermons? That was unheard of. So unusual that I had to see who dared. I traced the voice to the edge of the square, where festival chaos hushed him. Atop a rough wooden crate stood a young man in robes the color of sunlight and sky. He looked too young for the role, skin unmarred by guilt or tragedy. His arms fanned outward, palms open like offerings. He spoke with the fluid precision of a practiced rhetorician—verses of Torm and kin, woven into his cadence as though engraved on his soul.

But something wasn't right.

His confidence was unsettling. Too clean. Too guided. I watched his eyes: certain, compelling, except they drifted when they should have held me. The words rolled off his tongue too deliberately, like reciting a speech rather than feeling it. I leaned forward, curious. A sermon this public should ring with sincerity. Instead, his rhetoric cracked in places, half-truths slipped in among the verses. I saw them tumble over each other, eager to be heard, whether they meant what he said or not.

The crowd didn't seem to notice. They drank every word. Because whether he believed it or not, they did. And I realized... that was worse.

He spoke of Torm as though He were a neighbor. A companion. As though they shared meals and secrets and the sword of truth was some polished relic you could hoist above your head like a festival prize. His version of Torm offered no weight, no sacrifice. Only warmth. Certainty. As if conviction were a comfort, not a cost. That was not how we spoke of Him.

I looked at the crowd—wide-eyed, rapt, their faces soft with awe. They clung to his words like children at a puppet show, too dazzled to ask who pulled the strings. They didn't know his name yet. But they would. The shape of adoration was already forming in their eyes.

Something shifted beneath my ribs. A frigid pinch, like someone was wringing out my lungs. I'd stood in enough chapels to know what reverence felt like.

This wasn't that.

As his final words dissolved into the bright din of bells and barter, he looked at me. Held my gaze. And smiled. It wasn't just confident. It glittered. That was a smile built to sell things. The kind that made you feel singled out, special, like you alone had been offered a secret truth. That too warm, too knowing look was bait on a gilded hook.

Then he stepped down from the crate and vanished into the sea of bodies. No hurry. Just... gone. Swallowed by the swell of movement and adoration, as though the crowd had been rehearsing their whole lives for the moment they'd get to carry him.

I moved after him. I had to. Had to know who he was. Where he'd learned those verses. What had been bent inside them. I leaned forward, slipping between shoulders and shawls, murmuring half-apologies as I tried not to shove. He was pulling ahead.

Then—something hit. Hard. Somewhere nearby.

A sickening, meaty crunch. Metal on flesh, but with weight behind it.

My body stopped before my mind did. Breath caught mid-step.

I knew that sound too well.

Somewhere past the wind-chimed stalls and colored pennants, above the bell-choirs and sugar vendors, something had turned. It had already gone wrong. I gave the crowd one last look. Still clustered, still radiant, still spellbound. I turned and ran toward the sound, the pit already tightening in my stomach.

No sign of Luna. Or the other children. Good. Let them keep dancing. Let them not see this.

4 - Aurelian Vale

I turned the corner as the crowd began to peel away, some with narrowed eyes and shaking heads. Others watched with the kind of morbid curiosity that makes you ashamed of being human. And in the center of it all was Eryndra.

The white of her wrappings had dulled to a battlefield gray, smeared with city dust and someone else's blood. But the light beneath still leaked out in sharp, uneven beams—jagged like broken mirrors. Her shield was raised. Always raised. Always ready.

One man was already down, dragging himself through the churned dirt with a broken lip and a rapidly swelling eye. The other two circled like dogs who'd caught a lion by accident. Green, uncertain, feinting in that nervous way that tells you they've never fought anything but fear and themselves.

Eryndra wasn't even winded. If anything, she looked annoyed. Insulted. Her next blow caught the taller one square in the ribs. He dropped with a groan, and before the third could retreat, she clipped him across the face. A crack of cartilage. Blood a brushstroke across iron.

"Eryndra!" I called, pushing past a knot of onlookers. "Stand down."

Her body stilled, but only just. The third man staggered back, clutching his face. She turned partway—enough for me to see her expression. That mask of cold purpose. Her radiant profile caught the sunlight like a sculpture that had learned violence.

I moved quickly now, dread building behind my ribs. This wasn't de-escalation. This was spectacle. Justice as a cudgel. And I had the sinking feeling it had been going on for a while.

As I made my way to her, the three young men tripped over one another, scrambling into the nearest alley like kicked dogs. The crowd, assured the violence had passed, began to disperse, some shaking their heads, others already turning back toward the laughter and bells as though the blood in the dust had been part of the show.

How often had this become their entertainment? How long had discipline turned into demonstration?

I'd been gone too long. Eryndra didn't do this for pleasure—but she didn't shy from it either. And without someone to temper her…

My hands clenched. Rarek hadn't just drifted while I was away. It had sunk.

Like Kirtana, Eryndra didn't flinch in the face of threat. But unlike Kirtana, who used her grace to dissolve or redirect, Eryndra met it head on. Raised her chin, took a bite, and made herself taller than the opposition.

She turned without ceremony, marched to the edge of the square, and dunked her shield into the fountain with a solid splash. Water sloshed over the rim. Red bloomed in the basin like ink in milk.

"That fountain's meant for drinking," I said, too weary to put the full force of reprimand behind my words.

She scoffed, jerking the shield once, hard, to rinse away the last of the grime. "They let their children splash through it like it's a summer pond. Beggars bathe in it. Drunks clean their vomit. I saw a man wash his feet in it just this morning. They climb on it with their idiotic paper flags, hooting like apes." She shook her head, sneer deepening. "It's symbolic, so naturally they have no respect for it."

I stepped closer. "Otherizing them won't ease the tension. And punishment won't earn their respect."

"I don't need their respect, brother," she snapped, eyes flaring as she jabbed a finger into my chest. "I demand their obedience. I am the guard. I am the city."

"Do the rest of the guard approve of your methods?"

That stopped her. Just for a second. Her shoulders dipped, just barely, but it was enough. The great iron slab she called a shield sagged in her grip—suddenly, unmistakably heavy.

"You can't keep doing this, Eryndra..." My voice was low. It carried the weight of too many years, too many moments like this. "We're already treated like relics. Like curses barely tolerated. You know that. We have to speak our prayers in quiet. We hold our rituals behind closed doors. You think violence is going to fix that? You think bruises will make them listen?"

Her tension reignited, the fire returning to her eyes. "We shouldn't have to hide in the chapel, Daelon. We were made to preach, to sing, to protect! We shouldn't have to cover ourselves for the sake of these thankless, unenlightened fools!"

Her gaze snapped to the side, fixing on the last gawking bystander lingering sheepishly at the edge of the square. Her whole body seethed toward him with thunder in her stride.

"And what are you looking at?" she roared.

Before I could move, she ripped back the wrappings around her mouth. A blinding torrent of golden light tore from her, searing across the square and into the man's eyes. He screamed, dropping his festive banner, clawing at his face as he staggered and bolted blindly toward the noise of the crowd.

She drew the cloth back over her mouth, the last embers of the light retreating behind the linen mask. I stood frozen.

Of course our light could burn. We all knew that. But she'd *wielded* it. Out of fury. And with the crowd watching… gods, she'd given them something to be right about.

They already thought us sanctimonious. Thought we looked down from some pulpit none of them had the means or will to reach. But they hadn't reason to fear us.

Until now.

She stormed toward the spot where the man had fled, fury etched into every step, and crushed the fallen banner beneath her boot. The wooden staff snapped in two.

And yet… beneath the anger, beneath the blaze of her wrath, I saw it. The sorrow. It clung to her the way guilt clings to blood. She wasn't just angry. She was heartbroken. And this was how she showed it. I stepped closer and laid my hand on her shoulder. Beneath the linen, I could feel the tension wound tight as coiled wire.

"Eryndra Caelux," I said softly. "The Shield of Heaven."

She froze, every muscle rigid, as though my words might calcify her where she stood.

"You are supposed to protect these people," I continued. "Not fight them."

She tore away from me like a struck match, spinning on her heel. "I'm supposed to protect *our* people, Daelon!" Her voice cracked. She thrust an accusing finger toward the distant crowd of the festival. "*Those* are not our people. They don't need protection from us," she shouted. "We need protection from them!"

Her eyes burned, too bright. "They parade around in our symbols like trinkets. Mock our vows, and then spit when we hold them to it. You think I don't see how they look at us? How they sneer?"

She turned again, shaking her head. "Kirtana still thinks beauty will win them back. But they don't want truth. They want costumes. They want comfort. When we stop being useful—they'll turn on us. We have to show them we're not going to be trampled on!"

Her hand dropped. Her voice wavered. She stood there trembling, trying to hold the shape of her anger like it was armor, as if breaking meant losing.

I didn't say anything else. I just stepped forward and pulled her into a hug.

She didn't move at first. Didn't melt or soften. Just stood stiff in my arms, trembling, still clutching that massive slab of iron like it was all that held her together. Then she began to cry. Silent, shaking sobs. No collapse. No comfort. Just the release of something that had been building far too long. She didn't cry like someone asking for help. She cried like a fortress springing a leak. Quiet and furious, even at herself.

Her glow beat against me like an erratic war drum. I could feel it beneath the linen: not the calm tide of sacred light, but something wild, desperate. Scorching, not warm. It struck like a hammer on anvil, echoing off the edges of her body, raw and unresolved. My sister was fraying. Held together only by the sheer force of her will, by a faith so rigid it would rather burn than bend. I had not seen it. Had not wanted to see it. But now, wrapped in her light and grief, I knew.

This was my fault.

I should have stayed. Should have stood beside her, tempered her fury, steadied her flame. I should have held the line with Kirtana, lifted the weight she now bore alone. Instead I'd spent the past two years chasing phantoms. Following the whispered trace of our creator in hopes that their wisdom might lead us through this era of decay before any more of us turned away from our faith. Now I was tending to a fae child who slipped through my arms like water through lattice.

I'd been searching for some sacred answer to our problems. But maybe what was sacred had stayed behind. And I had left it.

I worried for her. That kind of tension doesn't dissipate; it builds. But she would never let me carry it for her, no more than she would let me carry that coffin lid she called a shield. Despite its weight, she clung to that slab like it was the only thing keeping her afloat.

I drew back, just enough to meet her eyes. "Your work here is done, Eryndra. Go. Kirtana's in the chapel. She'll be waiting."

For a moment, she didn't move. Her jaw flexed, shoulders still taut beneath the linen. She nodded, just once, and turned without a word. The shield sagged at her side, its weight no longer an extension of her fury, but a burden she had to carry. I watched her go, her figure retreating like a storm cloud passing behind the hills, quiet but spent. When she disappeared, I exhaled slowly. The street had calmed again.

I turned toward the square where I'd first seen him: the bright-robed preacher with the too-perfect smile. If there was a trail, I'd follow it. I had to know who he was. What he wanted. And why, when he spoke of Torm, I felt cold.

The sun had started to crest down from its zenith by the time I made my way through the outer quarters, my feet rapping faintly against the cobbles. The scent of fried sugar and roasted nuts lingered in the alleys, trailing behind bands of drunk revelers. I kept my eyes open, scanning knots of children for green hair, noting fountains and food stalls where Luna might have gone to gawk or steal a sip, but I didn't see her. Kirtana's assurance echoed in my mind, but it did little to ease my unrest. I wanted to *know* she was safe. But I couldn't afford to split my focus now.

The crowd that had swallowed the preacher had long since dissolved, their wide-eyed awe diluted into the aimless wandering of festival cheer. I passed a pair of vendors from that square, their faces familiar, voices raised now in haggling rather than praises. They had reintegrated into the fervent buzz, their fascination gone. Whatever metaphorical spell he'd cast had broken.

That was what chilled me. How easy it had been. No pyrotechnics. No miracles. Just a handsome man on a box, reshaping doctrine with a silver tongue and a knowing smile. They listened. They nodded. They believed. And for what? Empty theater. Style without soul.

It didn't make sense. I kept waiting for the real answer to reveal itself—for the hidden enchantment, the whispered compulsion, something. But as I passed through the square, there was no evidence of anything supernatural.

I turned a corner into a narrow colonnade and spotted him slipping out through a half-hidden side door carved into the wall of the library. It was an entrance few noticed, and even fewer used. Even with his preacher's robes swapped for simple breeches and a faded linen shirt, there was no mistaking him. The way he held himself, the tilt of his chin, the subtle curl of auburn hair at his temple: all unmistakable. And yet there he was, blending into the quiet, away from adoring eyes.

He carried a thick vellum-bound book and a few rolled scrolls under one arm. When he stepped into the narrow courtyard garden, stone benches and clipped box hedges shielding from the festival's clang, I caught up to him, unhitching the heavy silence I'd carried since the sermon.

"Excuse me," I said softly. He paused, turning.

"I hoped we might talk," I continued, meeting his eyes. "There's something I'd like to understand."

He studied me for a moment—neither startled nor unprepared, but measured. Then he offered his right hand. A gesture of civility. A handshake.

I hesitated, but took it.

His skin was cold to the touch, like an old woman on her death bed. But it was smooth, bearing no calluses or wrinkles. I felt the weight of centuries in that touch. It coated my senses with something that set every nerve on edge.

"Aurelian Vale," he stated with a small, polished smile of perfect ivory teeth. My skin crawled. "Come, let's walk."

He released my hand and adjusted his hold on the book. I followed him down a gravel path that curved away from the fountains and performers. Then he turned and motioned toward a secluded pair of benches tucked beneath a shady ghaf tree. Bells tinkled faintly in the distance, mingling with laughter, but a breeze blew toward the square, drawing the festival further away. Here, the air tasted quiet and urgent, like a confession paused on the tongue.

I seated myself across from him on the opposite bench beneath the tree. His smile, unsettling in its brightness, never wavered as I cleared my throat.

"Tell me," I began, "Who are you? Where did you come from?"

He leaned back, the book resting in his lap. His fingers tapped its cover with unhurried precision, as though each movement had been practiced in secret.

"I am a scholar," he said. Light glinted off the smooth skin of his hands. Hands that should have worn the marks of study, but were unnervingly pristine. "A humble seeker of knowledge, and a spreader of good will. I come from Talakit." He gestured down the path, as if the stones themselves were part of his tale. "A place known for its libraries and universities. I've traveled to Rarek to expand my horizons, to drink in the rich culture and history that flows through these streets."

Another lie. Rarek wasn't known for either of those things. Like in his sermon, every syllable felt rehearsed. Cheap. I held my silence for a moment, watching him. My gaze lingered on the chiseled slope of his jaw, the perfect smoothness of his skin. He was old enough to need to shave, but there was no sign of stubble nor trace of a razor's touch.

"Why preach Torm?" I prodded.

"Because the people want it." He tapped the thick vellum under his arm. "I bring the words. I bring understanding."

"Then why—" I hesitated, trying not to turn up my lip, "—why do you depict Him this way? Nothing in the scripture supports your interpretation. How could a learned man make so many mistakes?"

His eyes lingered on the book, then turned back to me. "I'm still learning—studying the verses, refining the sermons. I may get a point or two wrong. But I correct the parts they do not wish to receive."

His confidence grated against me. He hadn't said he corrected *his* mistakes.

"You mean to say you tailor the truth. Twist the verses into whatever shape makes them easier to swallow."

"Truth," he said, "is not a single, fixed blade. It is flexible, a set of tools, interpreted and applied."

"No." I shook my head, firm. "Truth, like Torm, is absolute. We do not edit virtue because it is unsavory."

An ancient hatred poisoned his face for such a brief instant I could have imagined it. Then his composure returned, smoother than before. "People rarely seek truth. They seek comfort. Certainty. Belonging."

"If your scholarship is earnest," I said, holding my tongue, "reread the scripture. And if you find yourself uncertain, visit the chapel. Speak with Kirtana. She is the truest voice of Torm in Rarek. You could learn much from her."

He tilted his head as if weighing something larger than the offer. His silence stretched, as though he were mentally counting out coins. The light through the ghaf branches painted him in shifting patches, and for a moment, I imagined I could see the real man underneath—coiled, calculating.

Then he blinked, and the scholar returned. "Yes," he said. "Yes, I most certainly will. Any guidance and knowledge on how to please the people would certainly be of value to me."

'Please the people.'

I swallowed my instinct to object. We both stood, knowing this conversation was over.

He extended his hand again. I took it.

Cold, like something preserved too long.

'Let her see through him,' I prayed. Kirtana needed to hear of this. She'd know what to do; she always did.

As our hands parted, a single leaf drifted down between us, twirling like an afterthought. Aurelian caught it effortlessly, his fingers closing around it with a care that felt almost ceremonial.

His gaze rose to the tree, the dappled light catching on the sharp edge of his cheekbone. "The ghaf is originally from Talakit," he said, his voice soft with a mock-reverence. "Its leaves are said to symbolize the victory of good over evil."

Then he looked at me.

The curiosity in his eyes vanished, swept away by that same restrained smile: the one that knew too much and chose to say too little. He tucked the leaf behind his ear, the gesture too neat to be careless.

"It's nice to see one here in Rarek," he added, then turned and walked off down the path, his steps slow, assured, untroubled. Like a man who believed the city already belonged to him.

5 - Uncertain Future

I turned my steps toward the chapel, Aurelian Vale's silver-tongued sermon still stirring up my mind like spoiled soup. The words clung to me, saccharine and sour all at once, their false sweetness leaving a film on my tongue.

Before I could reach the courtyard path, a flash of motion pulled my gaze. Purple and green streaked past, a blur too vivid to be anything but Luna. She darted into a nearby alleyway, bare feet slapping stone. A heartbeat later, two city guards barreled through the crowd in pursuit.

"Stop that girl!" one bellowed.

"She's a thief!"

My stomach sank. I broke into a run, turning sharply at the next street, hoping to cut them off. Whatever Luna had or hadn't done, I refused to see her in their hands. Despite Rarek's rainbow of faces and cultures, the guard remained stubbornly human. Stone-eyed and suspicious of anything not bred from their stock. Their tolerance for fae was thin on a good day.

I'm still not sure if they hired Eryndra to save face or because someone owed her a favor and feared a broken jaw. Either way, she was the outlier, an armored smokescreen to distract from the rot behind the sigil.

As I rounded the corner, Luna gasped and skidded to a stop, her heels scraping hard against the cobblestones, peeling slivers of skin from her calloused feet. She seemed like she'd been chased a mile, her tiny chest heaving. Her eyes looked like twin grapefruits sunk in a mask of fear. She clutched something tight to her chest, wrapped in stained burlap and panic.

I slowed, lifting both hands, palms out. "Woah! It's okay, it's okay. What's going on?"

She started crying. Quiet at first, the way children do when they're trying not to, as if making a sound would seal their guilt.

"No, no, no," I said gently, taking a careful step forward. "You're not in trouble. I just want to know what's happening."

She backed up, shaking her head, shoulders trembling. Still sobbing. Still clutching whatever it was like she would vanish if she let it go.

"What have you got there?" My voice stayed even, soft. But she wouldn't let me close. Wouldn't let me see.

Then came the whisper, so hoarse I barely heard it: "I wanna go home..."

My chest cracked.

"Okay, okay," I murmured, hands still outstretched, heart breaking. "I'll take you. Where is it?"

"I DON'T KNOW!" she screamed, her voice like shattered glass. Her eyes flared—red, crimson. The tattoos on her skin came alive, lifting like leaves in a storm, rustling and glowing, the red light running laps around her body. She writhed as the smell of smoke and burning flesh overtook the alleyway.

Behind me, the guards were still coming. I had maybe seconds. I didn't have time to think. No room for doubt. I scooped her up, gently as I could, and cradled her against my chest. The heat from the magic seething across her skin was unbearable, scorching through the linen of my chest and arms. I could feel it searing. But I didn't let go. She was still screaming, a dagger plunging into each of my ears.

Whatever she'd taken, she clutched it like her life depended on it. I couldn't even see it beneath the folds of cloth and terror.

A guard rounded the corner just as I turned, his boots thudding against the stone. Another came from the other end of the alley. Trapped.

"Hand over that thief, ethereal!" the first one barked, drawing a short sword. His eyes weren't on her. They were on me.

"Please," I said. "She's hurt. I'm sure there's an explanation that can wait—"

"Justice doesn't wait," the other spat from behind me.

"She's a child!"

"She's a criminal!"

Their weapons rose in tandem. The air was thick with heat and screaming and the stench of burning cloth. Luna convulsed in my arms, her whole body glowing like a brand.

They advanced. Heavy steps over the cobble. My mind raced with calculations and contingencies, none of them good.

My arms suddenly slapped against my chest. The burning stopped.

I looked down, stunned, as the seared linen gave off wisps of smoke. My arms were still lifted, still curved inward like a cradle, but they held nothing.

I caught the flicker of movement just to my side. Luna surged up from the ground, a blur of limbs and hair, and dove straight into the stone wall. Not against it—into it. The surface charred as her red hot skin vanished inside it like a ghost.

But her hands, still wrapped around whatever she'd taken, lagged behind. They hovered a second, resisting the wall's indifference, her knuckles taut, straining. As she pulled harder, her fingers slowly peeled open. The object slipped free and dropped to the ground with a faint clink as the last of her vanished into the stone.

A coin. Bright, decorative. One of the countless festival tokens handed out like sweets. Worth a few coppers, if that. Etched with smiling suns and dancing figures, mass-forged and forgettable.

This was what had drawn the chase? This was the cause of all that terror?

The guards advanced, their stares stuck to the burn marks on my chest and the space Luna had disappeared into. I stooped and picked up the coin. Thin, forgettable, its bright stamped faces grinning up at me like this was all a joke.

I held it up. "This?" I asked, my voice low, scorn barely withheld. "A child runs scared through your streets, and your first instinct is violence… over a trinket worth less than your boot polish?"

The foremost guard squared his shoulders. "A thief is a thief. Doesn't matter the sum. Holiday or not, scum doesn't get a free pass."

A fire ignited within me, raw and righteous. "Remembrance is about *sacrifice*," I snapped. "About *restraint.* About the gods giving up power, pride, *everything.* You'd think even a trash-peddling merchant, sullying the name of the day, might suffer missing pocket change without calling down the guard like she'd looted the treasury."

I flung the coin. It struck stone with a metallic tick and skittered across the cobbles to settle at the guard's feet. "There. Your great loss restored."

The two exchanged a glance. One looked at the wall, eyes narrowing, then back at me. Whatever they saw, or didn't, seemed to sap the wind from their sails. With a grunt and a shake of his head, the lead turned and moved off, his partner trailing.

Alone again, I looked to the wall.

A scorch mark, faint but undeniable, marred the stone. The place where she'd passed through. The answer to the mystery of the wagon. Of the crowds. Her limbs and frame moving through the world like breath through a sieve. She could phase. And she'd done it again: left me, like smoke curling through my fingers.

My hand rose of its own will, pressing softly to the warm patch where she had vanished. I felt foolish, knocking as if it were a door, hoping she might be hiding on the other side rather than fleeing at breakneck pace. "Luna?" I murmured.

No answer.

She could be anywhere now.

Back at the chapel, Eryndra had resumed her post by the shrine, arms crossed, eyes fixed straight ahead. She stood like a stone sentinel, daring anyone to come too close or linger too long. Whatever softness had momentarily stirred in her was now buried again beneath steel and scripture. The two elderly worshipers were gone—perhaps already seated at their home table, sharing old stories and modest food to honor the proper traditions.

Kirtana drifted quietly between the pews, adjusting a ribbon that had slipped, brushing dust from a sill with the side of her wrapped hand, coaxing the dirt on the floor along with a broom.

"A blessed hush," I said as I stepped into the aisle.

I looked down, suddenly aware of the soot and alley-grit likely on my heels. Too late. The runner beneath my feet bore the smudge of my passage.

"I'm sorry," I said, embarrassed.

Kirtana turned just enough to glance my way and shook her head with a gentle wave of her hand, as if to say, *You're always welcome, dirt and all.* She paused her sweeping, turning slightly toward me. "You only just left. Why are you back?"

I stepped closer, lowering my voice to match her tone. "Aurelian Vale," I said. "That's his name."

"Who?"

"A man preaching in the square."

"Preaching?"

She stilled, and I told her everything. How I'd found him, how he'd spoken Torm's name like it was a parlor trick, how his sermons stirred the crowd more deeply than even her songs. I told her of his smile, his calm, the way he twisted scripture with careful, pleasing words. How he called himself a scholar but knew Rarek's culture only through secondhand stories. How he claimed the people *wanted* Torm, not truth, not faith, but comfort.

Kirtana listened in silence, her eyes downcast but alert, sweeping her fingers once more across the worn grain of a pew. At the shrine, Eryndra remained still. Her posture betrayed nothing, but I could feel her listening, the way stone listens to a storm. Her arms were crossed again, but her fingers drummed once, twice, against the curve of her bracer.

"I asked him to come here," I admitted. "To learn from you. To hear the real verses."

Still, neither of them spoke.

"I don't trust him," I said. "His interest didn't seem to be in the scripture."

Kirtana nodded, slow and knowing. "We welcome all citizens and patrons of Rarek," she said gently. "If he is allowed to walk the city, he is allowed to walk here."

"As long as he doesn't muck up the shrine," Eryndra cut in from the front of the hall, her tone flat as the stone beneath her boots.

Kirtana shot her a look. Nothing dramatic, just a shift of light beneath the linen, but Eryndra was silent. She had said her piece.

I called them sisters, but the likeness stopped at light and language. In truth, we were all separate lines to the same forgotten verse. Besides our fading worship of Torm, we shared very little. And even that had begun to take different shapes. Kirtana folded her heart into her voice, cautious and deliberate, while Eryndra wielded hers like a torch in dry brush, reckless and emotional. I simply stood where I was placed, hoping that was enough.

Kirtana turned back to me, her gaze softening. "There's something else troubling you," she said. "Something more than a simple charlatan."

I hesitated, but only for a breath. Then I told her everything. About Luna. The chase, the heat, the burns, the phasing, the coin, the screams. How she'd disappeared into the wall.

As I spoke, Kirtana's expression remained still, but present. Listening the way only she could: fully, quietly, without judgment.

Aurelian Vale disturbed me. But Luna? Luna scared me in ways I couldn't explain. And still, all I wanted was to find her again. To protect her from whatever haunted her. Even if it meant chasing a ghost through walls.

Kirtana sighed, the sound barely more than a breath. "If she can phase through buildings," she said, "she'll have no trouble staying clear of the guards. But you can't go looking for her, Daelon. Someone with that kind of ability... if she doesn't want to be found, she won't be. With those marks, she was likely a prisoner at some point. Who knows what things she's done to escape and stay free all this time?"

My expression stayed firm. She glanced toward Eryndra, who gave the faintest nod, still silent, still watching.

"We'll keep an eye out," Kirtana continued. "Both of us. But there's not much we can do in the short term."

Then, with a softness that nearly undid me, she placed her hand on my shoulder.

"If you need something to take your mind off it… perhaps you should visit the library. See if Stetson's turned up anything new on your creator," Kirtana said gently.

"*Our* creator," I corrected.

Her hand lingered a moment longer on my shoulder before sliding away. Then she turned, resuming her quiet task of straightening the already straight. Eryndra turned her head, avoiding my gaze.

"It's obvious how the two of you feel about it," I said quietly, eyes tracing the worn groove in the chapel floor. "But I can't let it go."

"We know," Kirtana replied without turning.

Eryndra just huffed, crossing her arms tighter. Kirtana shot her a sideways glance. It was clear that she had already reprimanded Eryndra for her attitude earlier. For all the long-term good it would do.

"We know it's important to you," Kirtana continued. "And we know you're disappointed that it isn't important to us. But we each have our own devotions, our own passions. Please, go and see Stetson. We'll keep watch for Luna."

The sun bled low into the horizon, draining Rarek of its brightest colors and leaving behind a softened wash of orange and blue. The pulse of the festival had slowed like a great beast growing tired. Merchants folded up their wares with half-eaten sweets tucked into the folds of cloth, children who had flooded the streets with laughter were now ghosting back into the cracks they'd come from, and only a few diehards still clanged their handbells, more out of habit than joy.

No sign of Luna. No sign of Aurelian. No sign of the guards who had barked so boldly hours ago.

I made my way through the cooling streets, past piles of discarded streamers and the slow hiss of guttering lanterns, until the squat form of the library rose into view. It had no banners, no decorations, no clamor. I pushed the heavy wooden door open. It gave reluctantly, like a secret resisting being told.

Inside, the hush was absolute. Dust floated like memories between the stacks, but the floor looked like it had been swept recently. There was a thin smell of recently-burnt incense. But no visitors, no voices. Just the quiet patience of knowledge waiting to be asked for.

Stetson was exactly where I expected him to be: slumped in his creaking wooden chair behind the library counter, a half-shelved tome lying forgotten across his lap. His snores rose in sync with the slow rise and fall of his chest, more rhythmic than the handbells still clattering faintly outside.

"Stetson," I said softly, as I stepped closer.

No response.

I approached the counter, leaned forward, and gave it a firm tap with my knuckles. Still nothing. His head lolled to one side, breath rasping through his lips. I sighed, unwrapping my hand just enough to let a sliver of light touch his face. He squinted, scrunched up like a cloth caught in the wind, and slowly brought one hand up to rub at his eyes. The light winked out as I rewrapped my hand.

"Back from the dead, are you?" I said.

"Daelon," His voice croaked like a floorboard. "Quite rude to interrupt somebody's sleep… not like you'd know anything about that." Stetson blinked the rest of the haze from his eyes and sat up, bones creaking along with the chair. "Been what, a year now?" He sniffed. "Long enough the mice started thinking you were a myth. Back to enjoy the festival, are you?" he finished sarcastically, pulling the cotton out from his ears.

I gave a slight frown. "The lead turned cold. If a shrine was there, there's no trace of it now."

He sighed through his nose. "Figures. But at least there's still that last one."

"Let's see it then."

"Right to the point, as always." He leaned back, one hand absently scratching his jaw. "Look, I don't know what great spiritual epiphany you think you're gonna find out there. But if you're still set on it—"

"You know that I am."

He thumbed his nose at me. "Then I'll help where I can."

With a grunt, he pushed himself to his feet and shuffled off behind the counter, rifling through a stack of parchment, then stepping toward one of the older, dustier cabinets. "Hold on. Let me get the map."

He disappeared into the narrow stacks, grumbling softly as he shuffled behind the rows of bound vellum and faded ink. From the hollow quiet of the library, I raised my voice just enough to carry.

"So," I called out, "you still pretending to catalog all this dust?"

A muffled harrumph came from the shelves. "This dust is historical, I'll have you know. And I'll pretend a great deal more if it keeps me out of trouble with the city council."

"You could come by the chapel sometime," I offered. "Kirtana's still there. Eryndra too, if you're feeling brave."

"No need to go stirring old coals," he replied. "Torm doesn't need me blundering around in vestments I've long since outgrown."

"You didn't outgrow them. You just took them off."

A pause. "And you're still wearing yours like a badge despite them behaving more like shackles."

I let that hang in the silence for a moment. "Maybe. But at least they still fit."

There was no bite in his voice when he answered. "And I'm glad you've still got the spine for it."

A rustle of parchment, then his voice drew closer. "Found it. Don't laugh at how it looks. This map's older than me and twice as senile."

Stetson returned a moment later, the old scroll clutched beneath one arm, a few brittle pages balanced atop it. He cleared a space on the counter with one sweeping motion, then unfurled the parchment map, its edges curling from age and disuse. With delicate fingers, he spread out the accompanying papers, weighing them down with a trio of mismatched candle stubs.

"There," he said, tapping a faded ink circle just north of a range of hills. "Says there was a shrine here. Tormite. Remote. Abandoned or forgotten, most likely." He adjusted one of the loose sheets and tapped the date scrawled near the bottom. "Quite some time ago."

"Sixty years," I murmured. "Stetson, I'm only forty."

He gave a dismissive grunt. "Just 'cause the last record's sixty years old doesn't mean the place vanished the day after. Could've held on for decades. Could still be clinging by a thread." He leaned over, squinting at the map. "Point is, we've run out of newer leads. This is what's left. There might be one more, down here, but I'm still cross-referencing weak sources."

I traced a finger along the faded parchment, committing the two sites to memory. The first, our current lead, lay nestled just northwest, on a lone, easily-recognizable mountain. Close enough to reach without much trouble. The terrain would be steep, but likely unpopulated or at least civil.

The second mark sat farther southwest, its ink faint and worn at the edges, like a rumor that had lingered too long without proof. Far south of Rarek. South of even the marked settlements. Too close to Talakit for comfort.

Stetson didn't need to say anything. We both knew what that meant.

Rarek and Talakit weren't at war, not technically. But neither would claim the no-man's-land between them, and neither would lift a finger if something went wrong there. Just enough tension to keep the laws fuzzy, just enough pride to keep the wrong questions from being asked.

If that shrine turned out to be real, I could only hope the estimation was off by a few leagues—north, ideally. There was a stark difference between a long trip off the road and trespassing on land claimed by bandits.

Stetson gave a slow nod, rolling the map back up with careful, papery fingers. "I'll keep checking on that southern one," he muttered. "Wouldn't want to send you down into brigand territory without wringing out every other option first."

"I'd expect nothing less," I said, patting his shoulder as I turned toward the door.

"You're off already?" he called after me.

I paused, casting him a smirk over one shoulder. "Unless you're about to invite me for dinner."

He patted his round belly. "Share my food, with *you* of all people," he scoffed. "I mean to say that lead's not getting any colder than it already is. Maybe take a few days. Relax. Remind the city you still live here. That you're not just some wanderer, you know."

I turned back. The smirk faded. My hand slipped from the doorknob.

He squinted at me, motioned toward the kettle. "Well, don't just stand there. Come sit by the fire."

We sat. Just two tired men and a thin pretense of ceremony. The dampened roil of the festival outside outcompeted by the crackling flame before us.

"It all feels quieter now," I murmured, watching the steam coil upward from his cup. "The city. The chapel. Us."

He didn't look at me. Just ran a finger along the chipped rim. "You think I hung up my robes because I stopped believing?"

"I think you hung them up because people stopped listening."

That earned a bitter laugh. "Yeah. And I liked my teeth where they were. At the very least, it's given me some more time to read, and some more time with the ladies." He winked at me, saw I wasn't going to respond, then leaned back and looked around. "This place still gets a few visitors every now and then. Not like it used to. People don't seem that interested in reading anymore. The other Ethereals used to come in here all the time. All hungrier for knowledge than any scholar I've ever seen."

There was a long pause before he continued.

"The others didn't *all* go hollow, you know."

"I never said they did."

"No, but you think it." He sighed. "Most just got tired of being seen as… ornaments. The ones who stayed were mocked. The ones who left were forgotten."

I let that sit a while. Then: "Do you know where any of them went?"

"Far. And deep." He met my eyes for the first time. "They don't want to be found."

Neither of us said the rest. That those Ethereals who vanished had once shone just like I did. That it was easier to go dark than be judged for the light.

He cleared his throat. "You never stopped, though. Never even dimmed."

"I don't know how."

He nodded, slowly. "That's what scares them, you know. The people. You show them what they gave up."

"And what they could still be."

"Maybe," he said. "But that's not comfort. That's pressure."

Silence again, until he set his cup down and sighed.

I stood. "I should go."

I turned to the door, but said nothing. Because what was there to say? That I missed when we had more than memories? That I didn't want to be the last one shining?

A thought came to me as my hand touched the door.

"Have you ever heard of a place called 'Silverstrand Enclave'?" I asked, glancing back. "A place with sideways waterfalls, biting flowers, and a 'real sky'?"

Stetson's face twisted, brow folding in the middle like creased parchment. "Sounds like a child's fairytale."

"Look into it?" I asked. "For me?"

He studied me for a beat longer than usual. Whatever he saw on my face, it was enough to soften his skepticism. He gave a small shrug. "Suppose I will. Can't be too hard to find something that specific."

"Thanks," I said, nodding once more before finally stepping through the door and back into the cooling breath of evening. "Take care of yourself."

6 - The Weight of Expectation

The city no longer sang. Its voice had gone hoarse from cheer, leaving behind only the soft hush of wind pushing through forgotten ribbons. I walked the streets, my covered glow casting the only moving light between the hushed buildings. Vendors' stalls were packed. Crumbled pastries on the stone, the faint smell of burned sugar. Only the skeletons of celebration remained.

Candlelight pulsed behind windows, shuttered for privacy. The city had folded inward. Peaceful family dinners. Muffled conversations behind closed doors.

If only it were that simple.

It wasn't peace. It was pause. Not a day of Remembrance—just a day of forgetting. A day to light a candle and pretend it meant something.

I remembered when the streets had been lined with them. Rows of flickering light and bowed heads, the blessed hush of footsteps carrying prayers through the dark.

Now the candles were set on banquet tables, their wax catching crumbs and laughter.

The silence pressed closer as I walked. I had seen Rarek dressed in glory once. Now it all felt like a faded mural, painted over and forgotten. And maybe that was the truth. Maybe we were forgotten.

Not just us: the ethereals and the true Tormites. But the Right Hand himself. Torm. The virtue. The sacrifice. All of it, left behind by a world that had moved on. There hadn't been a new ethereal in… I didn't know how long. None that I'd heard of. None in Rarek. None on the road. Maybe my family were the last to be made.

The word toiled in the void between my mind and tongue, anxious that it might not be actualized. Family. Kirtana, Eryndra, and I were not born to a mother, not raised under a roof. We were conjured, woven from virtue and scripture. Delivered not through blood, but by faith.

I'd always known someone had written us. That a mortal hand had laid the first thread. Their creed and love written on the wrappings we were born in. But the further I walked, the more I wondered why. Why create a creature like me? Why reach so far past reason, past understanding, just to speak life into dust? Was it grief? Madness? Faith?

Or hope?

That was what the mountain shrine promised. This lead, tucked in the mountain, might be the last. Maybe, at the end of the trail, there'd be a reason. A name. Something to tell me that I hadn't been born into silence. That I hadn't endured all this for nothing.

The wandering. The cold nights. The eyes of strangers narrowing with suspicion. The long, tired silences between me and my sisters. I had pushed so far away from them, from this place, clinging to a promise no one else upheld. If I exhausted all of my leads, what would that make me?

Just a relic still pretending the world still needed one.

I settled onto a bench, its wood bowed from years and weather. My pack sat beside me, loyal and light. I unfolded its contents with slow, deliberate hands, more ritual than necessity. No food, no drink, but no need. My compass still pointed true. Ink, enough. Strips of linen, thin and frayed, but serviceable. The implements for documentation and repair remained. I would mark myself with scripture and memory, as always. Even if no one ever read it but me.

As I shifted, I caught sight of the burns. Thin, black rings where Luna's searing limbs had pressed against me. She had screamed with such force it seemed to split her small body open. I'd held her anyway. I would have let my story burn away completely before letting her go. But that wasn't my choice to make.

I traced one of the marks with my thumb. Not tonight. But soon, I would write about this. I'd have to. I had to make sense of it somehow. I always tried. Even if my words couldn't do it justice.

Somewhere far off, a shutter closed. Wood creaked. A child's laughter echoed once, then vanished. The hush returned.

There was no reason to wait until dawn. The shops would offer me nothing I required. The city's needs would continue with or without me. Prejudice would fester. Aurelian would charm or wither, Kirtana would shepherd, Eryndra would smolder. Luna would vanish deeper into shadow. My staying would not change the shape of any of it.

Still, it hurt to rise. Not in the bones, but somewhere under them. I stood, slung the pack over my shoulder, and turned toward the always-open gate. As I stepped forward, my boot caught on something hard, sending a bright clink against the stone.

A festival coin.

I stooped to pick it up. She'd clutched one as if it were the last anchor to her name. As if it had weight enough to tether her through an encroaching storm. The embossed sun, grinning madly above the half dozen other smiling faces. A family. She must have missed hers terribly.

'I wanna go home...'

I felt it again. My ribs tightening, crushing me the same way they had when she vanished through the wall. The same ache that left me frozen in alleys instead of moving. My heart demanding that I do more.

I walked the coin to the alley where she had disappeared. The stone was still dark with the ghost of her passage. With the smallest mote of hopeful insanity, I knocked again.

Silence answered.

I crouched, placed the coin at the base of the wall, and left it there. For her; in case she ever came back.

The next months slipped past like a distant song—one I could faintly hear but not know. Each morning was the same: my boots touched cold earth, and I whispered the word 'north'. My feet obeyed, and I followed. Rain soaked me. Wind lashed me. But those were simple tides to stride through. I did not need shelter, nor food, nor sleep to carry me forward. My body moved because it must, and with this constant movement, my mind churned as well.

I passed settlements that rarely even warranted a map's dot: moss-streaked stone huts, narrow lanes hemmed in thorn hedges, children trailing laughter behind them into empty households. Sometimes an old woman would peer through shuttered windows, studying me from a distance. A shopkeeper's eyes would flick to my wrapped face and glowing palms. They'd lean their heads together, whisper and shake them, as if I'd asked them to pray for snow. I would say nothing, and keep going. They had nothing I was seeking. No answers on how to save a dying faith. No gods to light the way and give me strength. No home to rest my spirit within.

The skies changed many times. Bright, scorching sun; stormclouds rolling in ragged gray; weekslong mists that soaked the linen on my arms. Nothing slowed me. Still, I would pause. Beneath a crag of granite or near a pool that didn't belong to any path, I would stop, gather kindling, and build a quiet fire. Set the light away from its coil. Let the stars burn overhead. Then I would stare into the fire, removing the wrappings from my chest and neck, until I could read them again.

People called them our skin, as if they were intrinsic, part of our form. But they weren't. Strip us of our wrappings, and you would still find a body beneath—one shaped like a person but lit like a furnace, leaking radiance from every crack. Most couldn't bear to look directly at us when we were bare. Some cried. Some screamed. Others whispered superstitions, called us angels or devils. But all turned away.

Those who didn't believe the cloth was fused to us thought we wore them for tradition, reverence, or humility. But that was also not the truth. We wore them because our unmasked selves frightened people. Hurt people. The light was not violent. But it was unfiltered, untamed, unflinching. And that was enough.

So we hid ourselves. Not because we would cease to be without them, but because the world needed us to. We wrapped our radiance in worn cloth, dulled the brightness until it was enough to pass, to not disturb, to make others comfortable. That was the mercy we offered: not changing who we were, but concealing it. Lowering the volume. Letting others believe they were seeing the whole, when in truth, they saw only what we allowed them to.

It wasn't a sacrifice. It wasn't even a burden. It was just... what was required. And yet... there were times I wished I could unlearn the courtesy. Strip myself bare and be received without recoil. Let someone, anyone, witness me without flinching.

But the world does not allow for such things. So I continued to wear my mask, not because I needed it—but because they did.

Yet this at least allowed me to wear the script.

It was called Celestial. Back before my time, when belief still held weight and the gods had not yet retreated behind silence, the language was said to have been bestowed upon the world by angels. I never put much stock in that story. Angels, after all, were a luxury of certainty. They didn't belong to faith. They belonged to evidence. If angels walked the world, leaving traces and answers and crisp truths, they would be studied, not worshipped. Measured, not mythologized. Religion would become philosophy, a practice of observation and repetition, not prayer. It would collapse under the weight of their facts, or contort itself to no longer need them, if it wished to survive.

And so, perhaps, it was better that they remained a story. A scaffold. A whisper sewn through generations of quiet uncertainty.

Still, the script itself held beauty. That much was undeniable. Each symbol wove curves and twists in deliberate measure, every stroke a quiet offering to a long-dead god. There were no sharp angles, no breaks or harsh corners—only graceful loops and fluid lines that seemed to speak even in silence. Each letter had its own balance, its own movement. A spiral for sorrow. A pair of parallel sweeps for devotion. A descending loop that meant 'endure'. Even the ink bled differently into the linen, soaking slow, as if savoring its role in the act.

None of it was wasted. Celestial wasn't like Common or Elvish, cluttered with half-pronounced consonants or crushed syllables. It was elegant. Precise. Written for those who had no room to be careless with their faith, known now by only the most devoted of scholars. Every line served a purpose. Inked prayers and desperate pleas; my creator demanding that I stand up for what was right and true. It was their faith, their conviction, that had brought me and my sisters to life.

There were moments when my hands grew restless with new ink, new lines to bind memory: tears shed at Luna's scream, the scorch of grief on my chest, the weight of Aurelian's false valor… I added them to my wrappings at the edge of the blaze. Each word was a whisper to the world: *"I was here. I am real."*

Occasionally a traveler would cross my path. A shearer bearing fleece, a lone pilgrim on a donkey, a child herding goats. They rarely asked my name. More often, eyes narrowed behind weathered smiles. One elderly teacher from a forest fringe asked if I could read them my script, they taught literature at the small village founded centuries past. I unraveled a few words on the linen and spoke them aloud, owning the story behind them.

This was the only benefit to wearing these trappings: sometimes a person would ask their meaning, and I would be gifted the opportunity to share a part of myself. Not just the part written into that length of cloth, but the piece the strip covered, as well.

Mostly, though, I walked alone. Where my thoughts could torture me.

I loathed my evasions: how I wished to carry the world's brokenness, yet ran from responsibilities I didn't consider important. How I invoked purpose like a weapon, but refused it when it was presented to me in some queer form. I didn't desire to *look* like a savior, or be treated like one, only to *be* one. For my internal sense of worth and purpose.

I envied how Kirtana gave care so easily. How the world let her. Even when it went unthanked, her kindness was received. People trusted her voice. They let it move them. She could cradle strangers in the soft silk of her presence, and no one questioned her motives. No one told her to stand back or be quiet or stop helping. But when I reached out, even gently, even with every ounce of grace I could summon, the reaction was almost always the same: refusal. Suspicion. Recoil. As if my help came with claws. Even Luna…

And Eryndra. Gods, I envied her callousness. Not for its cruelty, but for its clarity. No one looked at her and wondered what she meant, or whether she could carry them. Her strength was not up for debate, her motives never misinterpreted. She made space by stepping into it. But I… I wanted to be soft and strong. Gentle and immovable. A protector, not a warden. I wanted to ease burdens, not become one.

Yet even my own sisters didn't trust me. Not when it counted. Kirtana knew things would unravel and never warned me. Eryndra cracked and never let me hold the weight. If I wasn't good for that—if I wasn't good for *them*—then what was I for?

The mountain crept nearer each sunrise. Its peak above the tree line showed first, distant and pale. Then ridges, broken spires. Soon the valley where the lone peak rose in ragged assertion. Northwest. Above the foothills, on a slope of shale. Then maybe the shrine, or some whisper of it, would find me. And I would know my purpose had found footing again.

Still, the road ended just beyond campfires and star charts. I slept not, but lingered until dawn brushed the sky. Each night, I had the thought: *Why am I still here?* And each night, I answered: *Because I must.* For if I did not stand at that shrine, if I did not find the wisdom and courage to lead, then I feared I would have nothing left to bring home. Not even the faith I still wore in helixes of dulling ink.

So I continued. Montages of stone and sky and solitude. Of prayer and remembrance. I walked, because to stop now would mean I had ceased to be more than light and parchment, more than wandering stories and memory. And I refused to vanish.

At the base of the mountain, I tilted my head back and let my eyes trace the jagged ascent. The peak was distant, crusted in old snow and shrouded in a gray shawl of clouds. Somewhere along that vast incline was supposed to be a shrine. That was all I'd been given. A mountain, and a maybe.

It was always like this.

Yet I followed every foggy lead, mapping the imperfect imaginations of the long dead. A worn icon, a slab of scripture half-buried in earth. But they never belonged to Torm. Wrong language, wrong symbols, wrong sentiment, wrong century. Other times, the site had vanished entirely—if it ever existed. Torn down, perhaps. Or swallowed by the earth, buried by landslides, floods, and time. Or maybe it had never been real at all. Just words, spoken once, remembered poorly, and passed along until someone like me came looking.

A few times I had found a temple or shrine, still standing, that did indeed belong to Torm. Sometimes tucked in forest glades or carved into the sides of lonely hills, their symbols worn, but still legible to one like me. The worshipers—if any remained—had never heard of me, my sisters, or the one who breathed life into us. They called me a blessing. A marvel. Some wept. Ethereals, to most of them, were legend. Living scripture. Word-bound guardians whose existence proved the divine had not entirely left the world. But to me, I was a question.

And I asked it. Was there a record of my maker having been here? An account of an ethereal's birth? A story passed down of scripture come alive on this soil? But the answer was always no. If my creator had lived, worked, or prayed in those places, they would know. And they assured me that mark would linger like scent on a robe. There would be some unmistakable sign.

But there never was.

Often they asked me to stay. To lead their rituals. To lend their dwindling faith in Torm the gravity of my presence. Their joy at my arrival dulled when I made it clear I was looking for something specific, *someone* specific, and didn't intend on staying. I couldn't. Each time I left them behind, it carved a little deeper.

Because I wanted to stay. I wanted to give them sermons worth remembering, to remind them how to speak the verses with reverence instead of fear. I wanted to believe that each tiny, flickering hearth of belief could survive on its own. But if I let myself believe that one more desperate family was reason enough to stop searching, I would never find the answer I needed. I wasn't looking for lost sheep. I was looking for the shepherd who had willed me into being. The one who might still know the path back to the light.

My endless march toward answers continued. It is fortunate my body required no rest. My mind, however, would have welcomed a pause.

Still, I began the climb.

7 - The Loudest Silence

As I started my ascent, I felt it. The quiet. The stillness. The territorial eyes upon me.

Not from creatures, nor watchers. From the cold.

It did not whisper or howl. It watched. Waited. And when I crossed the line where soil gave way to brittle stone and snow-stung wind, it stirred. Not with speed or sound, but with presence. As if I had been trespassing long before my feet touched the frost.

Still, I climbed.

There was a shrine, they said. Hidden high in the wind-scoured spine. A remnant of something sacred.

I told myself I believed it. I made myself believe it. Because belief gave shape to motion. Because the thought of a place where Torm's name had brought life to scripture, was just enough to force the next step.

I ordered my limbs to move despite the stiffening of the wrappings around them, those waterlogged linens beginning to freeze and resist. I forced my steps to land evenly, to keep the cadence steady. I could feel ice forming in the creases. Little crystal daggers threading along the seams of my joints. I flinched at the bite of them. Not because I feared succumbing—my body would not perish from the cold—but because the pain was distracting.

The cold brought with it a silence I hated. The loudest silence that didn't empty the mind, but drowned it. Beneath its surface, the worst parts of me stirred. They whispered of failure, of futility, of the long road ending in an empty shrine, if one even existed here at all. Of my sisters growing tired of waiting. Of Luna—branded, abandoned, and starving—learning the same lessons I had. That the world had no place for people it didn't understand.

I hated that the cold extinguished the rest of my mind and gave those tiny voices room to breathe. To swell.

The mountain loomed, patient in its hunger. It did not demand. It *invited* failure. It *expected* it. But I would not oblige.

I did not answer to mountains.

I answered to the voice that lived beneath the ice in my chest—the one that told me to keep going, even when all reason told me there was nothing left to find. Even when all the old paths turned to frostbitten silence. Even when the only thing that changed was the shivering of my own consciousness. So I marched. Uphill. Into wind. Into snow.

And the cold kept watching.

Without daylight to mark direction, my progress blurred into whiteness and wind. Every flake became a wall, every gust a blindfold. Above me, the sky was lost to the storm. I had no stars to guide me. Only the pulse of conviction in my chest—my purpose—and that too grew faint as the chill crept deeper into my skull. If there was any mercy left in the world, it was here. Hidden. Waiting.

As I climbed higher, I could feel my light dimming under the mountain's scrutiny. The longer I climbed, the more each step consumed what little warmth I carried. The linen bindings around my limbs had frozen into matted, crystallized armor. Beneath the stiff fabric, my light began to flicker and gasp.

I stumbled over another featureless mound, the white haze immediately swallowing my footprints. Panic sharpened at the edges of thought: had I already been here? Where was *here*? The mountain had no memory of my steps, no signposts, no waymarks to confirm passage. Even the snow sneered at my presumption.

Pain pulsed in my wrists and ankles, where the ice gathered most fiercely. Each flicker of my inner light betraying an erratic beat, a hesitation, a sputter. I had seen it before: other ethereals going hollow. Their flames dimmed, tinted strange colors—scarlet, putrid green, moldy blue—flirting with the darkness before winking out completely. Eyes glowing at first with conviction, then as dull as spent stone. Some vanished entirely into prisons of ash and silence.

What if I'm next? The mountain only needed time; I needed purpose. My light wasn't my life force. It was what I carried: the belief that I had worth, that I owed something to the world and to myself. Losing it meant losing *that.* A shell might remain, but what then? What would become of me? Someone caught in that terrible nowhere could linger forever, entombed by ice in a body without life but without death.

I stopped. A frigid lump stuck in my throat. I fell to my knees and pressed both palms to the earth, to feel the rocks biting through the snow, unforgiving and raw. I closed my eyes, willing the radiance to return. To guide me.

To protect me.

I remembered Kirtana's light: songs that stilled the body but moved the soul. The way her voice carried not just melody, but mourning. How she wove our lost history into every note, not to relive it, but to remind people it had once been worth remembering. Her song was the temple when no stone stood. She gave them a way to believe again. I owed her. For every festival morning she stood alone, lifting joy from cracked pews and hollow hearts. For every moment she kept our legacy beautiful, even when beauty had stopped being profitable.

I remembered Eryndra's light: the strength to stop sieges both physical and spiritual. The weight of her shield as it crashed down on enemies and injustice. The way she turned her fury outward to protect the soft, because the world never had. The way she suffered for her ideals, even if she wore them like armor. I owed her. For every fight I didn't join. For every time I'd vanished into the world, chasing origins, while she fought to keep what little we still had safe. For every day she stood at the shrine like a statue of vengeance, unmoving and misunderstood.

I remembered Luna's light: the sparkling pink in her eyes and the searing red of her arcane shackles. Her bony limbs and unkempt hair, the way she flinched like a wounded bird, the way her tears carved trails through the dirt on her cheeks. The way she screamed because the pain had nowhere else to go. Her body was breaking under a world too cruel for her, and yet she still clung to life with such zeal. I owed her. For the child she used to be. For the one she might still become. For the possibility that someone, anyone, might finally reach her—and I had to be that someone.

These were the faces that pulled me back from the edge. Their hopes. Their grief. Their belief in me. They were the ones I carried up this mountain. They were the ones who kept me moving, even when my light dimmed.

My duty to them pulled me forward. But not even they were the core.

Beneath all that—below the hymns, the names, the weight of their needs—was something quieter. Meaner. More defiant.

It was me. My refusal to quit. My unwillingness to let the trail go cold. My need to *know*. To find the hand that made me, or the void where it should have been. To finish the question, even if there was no answer.

My duty to myself is why I was still alive. A stubborn inferno that refused to succumb.

The ache in my chest deepened. My heart twisted in on itself, coiling like a serpent trying to tie itself into a knot.

My heart...

I opened my eyes. The light had returned, brighter than it had been since I dared set foot in the cold's domain. It was back. I hadn't lost my way. I was being tested. And I would not be found wanting.

I loosed the bindings at my neck, letting a thread of linen float free and my glow to thaw a patch of ice. And I rose. The wind snarled, the cold desperate to maintain its hold that the silence hadn't kept, but I answered back with every step. The mountain would not guide me, but neither would it claim me. As long as I could hold this torch—it would lead me upward.

And so I climbed.

I wandered for days in that grinding white. Direction meant little. The sun, hidden behind the dark clouds, offered no warmth. Drifts pressed against battered stone; wind-lashed trails evaporated into mist.

Each time I thought I'd reached a new ridge, I found the same scarred trees, the same broken cairn swallowed by ice. I kept a tally in my head. Turns taken, paces stepped. But the cold stole those, too.

My compass wavered and jerked, pulled off-center by veins of iron in the rock. It spun like a lie in my hand, north turning into nothing. There were moments I wasn't sure if I was searching or circling. If I had missed the shrine, or if it had never been here at all.

The cold had settled in my bones. Night lingered in my ribcage, frost in my fingertips, icicles dangled from my jaw. And yet I did not bow.

Because I had to be right.

Because if this place was empty, then so was I. If the shrine didn't exist, then all of it—the searching, the silence, the absence from my family, the devotion to my faith—had all been for nothing.

My sisters still kept the faith. Their verses hadn't changed. But mine had become *unbearable* to them. I hadn't strayed. I hadn't wavered. Why did they speak to me like I had?

Rarek hadn't forgotten. But it wanted to. And those of us who still believed were the mirror it couldn't bear to look into. Memory was the sin, not apostasy.

That's why the shrine had to be here. Here, where nothing soft could survive. The cold preserved what time had ruined elsewhere. The unchanged, untouched truth would be buried in this place where nothing else could grow.

Then my foot caught.

I stumbled forward, nearly slamming face-first into the snow. I braced my palms, teeth gritting against the ache in my spine. Beneath me, something hard and angular refused to budge. My pride pricked: *You've almost broken yourself, you can't even walk right.* I turn around and began to scrape at the snow with my hands, numb to the ice slicing into me.

It was a pedestal. Taller than my knees, carved from the same gray-green stone as the mountain. A thin column, crowned with a flat disk that shone beneath the snow—something smoothed and shaped.

A shrine?

My breath caught. My heart stuttered. I crouched, clawing frigid flakes aside to clear the pedestal.

The symbol. Where was the symbol? I had to find...

My hands found a simple set of rings—two copper bands looped together like a chain, unbroken. A symbol of peacefulness hanging here, at the harshest throat of the world. A symbol not of Torm, but of a goddess of togetherness, connection, safety among people.

Here? At this height of loneliness? On this wind-bitten slope?

It should have been funny, a cosmic joke. A place where frost-bitten bodies sought refuge under the watch of a deity of gathering and hearth. *This* was what I'd found. *This* was the answer to the puzzle I'd chased: not the maker of my existence, but a shrine to *belonging* on a mountain of damning isolation. A place the goddess of families, of bonds, never should have been. It should have been ridiculous, but instead it was enraging.

Because *this* was not my purpose. *This* was not why I climbed.

And for the first time, the mountain had answered.

All that remained was two circles of copper, abandoned at the mercy of snow and wind, worshipped by no one, tethered to nothing. And the mountain, sadistic as ever, had chosen to leave me with that instead of truth.

No. I came all this way. I nearly collapsed under this damned cold. I'd been walking for *months.* This couldn't—*couldn't*—be what the account had meant by its description.

The looped bands glinted cruelly in the pale light. Like some mockery forged in metal. Denial clawed at me, desperate to stay contained. But the cold burrowed deeper, dulling reason, amplifying rawness. My heart pounded. The air froze on my tongue. My hands trembled beneath the ice, fists clenching.

I lashed out.

First, I smashed my throbbing hands into the cold stone. A snap as the twin bands detached from their vertical stand. I seized them, drawing them back over my head before bringing them down on the shrine itself. Another crushing blow. The rings groaned and bent, separating from their once-eternal embrace. I hurled them, one sliding downhill over bare rock, the other sank into the snow. My arms burned not from the cold anymore, but from outrage.

"Take your unity and choke on it!" I howled, voice swallowed by the mountain's choking void.

My ribs ached. My hands were bloody. I stood motionless, chest heaving, staring at the fractured shrine. And I realized, in that moment, how utterly alone I truly was.

The cold quickly stole what heat my anger had built. The air howled like something alive, that furious blaze snuffed by stripping wind and apathetic ice. I stood above the shattered shrine, fists trembling, knuckles raw and slick with frozen blood. The twisted bands lay keening in the snow—broken absolutes rendered meaningless.

I bowed my head. It hurt: the weight of what I had done. They didn't deserve this.

The pedestal had been silent before. Now it cracked under its own failure, stone splitting in an echoing hiss. My hands shook too badly to touch it. Even if I had the tools to straighten the metal loops, reforge their embrace, my hands would not obey. My fingers were frozen pillars of pain.

Nothing could set this right.

I pressed my palms to my face, hiding my tears from the biting wind.

No, no. I whispered it into the storm: *It's okay.*
This didn't have to be the end. It wouldn't be.
There was still one more lead.
One more chance.
I could still fix this. *It wasn't over.*

I clenched my jaw. I shook the snow from my cloak and swallowed the ache in my chest.

Even if all signs had failed me here, the horizon still pointed forward.

I didn't need clarity. I didn't need comfort. I just needed something *next.*

Let the bitter cold of these cliffs hide my shame. Let it keep what dignity I shattered here: my pride, my certainty, my restraint. I left them all among the broken bands of another silent goddess.

Not because I was free of them. Because I couldn't carry them anymore.

The path was no clearer than before, no warmer, no easier. But the light in my chest, no longer a trembling spark, held fast. The ache of this loss, a stubborn flame newly kindled, settled in beside my resolve.

And so I walked. Because I didn't know how to stop. Even as the deafening silence roared back in my face.

The first step off the snowpack felt like a confession of my failure. The brittle crunch of white gave way to damp earth. Brown grass peeked through the frost like something meant for someone else. Not for me. Not for what I'd become.

I began the long march back toward Rarek. The months stretched ahead like a map I didn't want to follow.

Time lost its shape. Weeks bled into each other. The rhythm of footfall and faded light replaced thought. I crossed valleys without noticing, passed streams without acknowledgement. The rage that had broken me on the peak had quieted, its memory a scream muffled under the snow.

And when sorrow crept in, I didn't fight it. I let it walk beside me.

The wind no longer cut, but the silence still followed. Gone was the spark that had driven me skyward, the thinned-out hope I'd mistaken for purpose. The cold had left me, but my hands still ached from holding on too tightly to nothing.

I was going home. Not to comfort, but to consequence. To a city where faith was spectacle and memory was mocked. Where my sisters would greet me with that same look—the one that said: *Why are you still doing this to yourself?*

Family I'd been away from too long. Accusations I had earned. Comforts I both craved and despised.

Comforts—there's a joke. Rarek's taverns would offer warmth at the price of spiritual frost. Its gaslight streets would blink at me like I was some ghost they weren't quite brave enough to exorcise.

I compared myself to Kirtana often. Her quiet strength was anchored not in force, but in patience. Each note from her voice a bridge, not a barrier. She held her tone not to strike, but to steady. In her, I saw the true power of restraint: how to guide without leading, how to criticize without guilt. I admired it deeply: her self control, that she never snarled at the world like I did. Every lash of bitterness, every hot word I hurled into crowds, was a confession I carried alone. She never snapped at the blindness of the people, never raised her voice to drown out theirs.

And yet people listened to her. They always had. They heard her songs and softened. They saw her and quieted. Not out of fear, but out of some reverence I couldn't summon in others. Not without a raised voice or a lit path. I never understood that. Why did her gentleness command more attention than my urgency? She let their ignorance wash over her, like she was above it—or perhaps indifferent to it. Kirtana walked through chaos unchanged, unmoved by doubt or rage... or so it appeared.

I wondered if she ever felt the specter of shame haunting her, if doubt ever darkened her quiet eyes. If it did, she never let it chart her course. Instead, she pressed purpose forward. Always forward. No fits of rage, no collapse of confidence. Just a determined truth. I respected that, yet envied it. How could someone so calm make waves in a world so jagged? Did she ever feel the tremor of her own conviction faltering? How was her clarity so consistent? She held us to our highest, and to our lowest. She fostered what I refused to nurture: grace, self-control, a willingness to believe there was more to faith than steadfast conviction.

I told myself I didn't want what she had: that calm, that poise, but still I measured myself against it. She never wavered. Didn't lash out. Never flinched. Some part of me admired her, truly. Another part despised how easy she made it look. As though faith, unshaken, could be worn like a shawl. It wasn't that easy. It couldn't be. I just wish she'd admit how hard it was. Then maybe I wouldn't feel like I was a failure for struggling. I saw in her a confidence I lacked.

And I resented her for it.

Eryndra, on the other hand, so fierce she could shatter stones with her bludgeoning glare. When she entered a room, it bent around her in deference. As if the air knew she was there to defend it. She was unshakable, uncompromising, and I both admired and loathed that about her. She didn't ask for space; she claimed it. Her steps carved paths, where mine always seemed to follow old ones.

Where she sometimes used violence as certainty, I poured at least as much force into nothingness. Into restraint, denial, and burying guilt. I wrapped my doubts in silence and told myself it was mercy. She swung her convictions like a hammer. I locked mine behind my teeth. Was that better? Or just a quieter war?

At least her motives were pure. They always had been. She defended the people, the relics, and the faith like a lone soldier holding the line to protect an entire kingdom. She had her purpose; knew it, owned it. I wished mine were as clear and simple. She was the bulwark, the guardian, the last line of defense. What was I? Some half-scripted thing still trying to define his title.

Somewhere, the thoughts shifted. The lens turned inward. It always did.

In the blank hours, those endless, dreadful afternoons, I replayed my sins. I saw myself smashing the shrine: the petty cruelty in the act, my need to annihilate something I couldn't claim. How often had I lashed out when I felt powerless?

I thought about how I hid in piety while spilling my fury into innocent stone.

Was my conviction not strong enough? My words not convincing? Did I falter in some unseen way, some flaw in the script of me? Was it my appearance? Did they see my emotions as weakness? Was it because I appeared male? It couldn't be racial prejudice, or suspicion of the supernatural. Eryndra and Kirtana were both ethereal, and they weren't received like this. They weren't *welcomed*, no, but even the scorn they received felt navigable. Bearable.

But me?

I was met with a different kind of refusal. Not contempt, not anger, not even distrust—just rejection. A slow, quiet turning away. Like I wasn't supposed to be there at all. I didn't understand it. And because I didn't understand it, I didn't think I could learn. So I would keep walking in circles. Keep offering hands no one would take. Keep feeling like I was born to help a world that no longer wanted help, at least the kind I was capable of giving.

And that chilled me more than any cold.

I considered Stetson's maps, worn and frail and full of promise. I hoped he'd found something—anything—about the shrine in that no-man's land between Rarek and Talakit. And information about the Enclave Luna supposedly hailed from, if it were anything more than a child's lullaby. Sideways waterfalls, biting flowers, a 'real sky'.

I trudged back through the sparse hamlets. Dust-crusted homes and bent field markers passed me by, indifferent. The roads were safe, the paths quiet. But the stillness offered no comfort. It gave me space to think.

And I did. Too much.

I thought about Luna, how she recoiled when I touched her, but not when Kirtana did. I couldn't tell if it something specific about Kirtana, or something specific about *me*. But when Luna pulled away, mistrust in her eyes, I felt the same dagger in my chest that her screams put in my ears.

Luna clung to scraps of belonging. That festival coin that nearly bent as she squeezed it, the tiniest comfort in the reminder of home. I ached for her. That sting... that pained cry from missing something... I *knew* what it felt like.

Because I was doing the same.

Clutching at a dying faith's rituals. Digging through ruins and whispers, looking for confirmation of the shape I felt myself to be. Not the one they saw.

My sisters found peace in their roles. They'd carved out space for themselves in Rarek, quiet and useful, tucked behind temple doors or beneath civic function. They were allowed that stillness. That duty.

I wasn't. Every time I came back, I was scrutinized. *Pitied.* No one ever let me just… be. Not as the person I *wanted* to be. Had there been some error in my verse? Some cosmic misspelling that muddied my role as messenger?

I was never convinced of my own holiness.

The old Tormites look at us like we're angels. Messengers. Incarnations. Not *people.* But I knew better. Angels were always easier to worship when they stayed in stories. I wasn't some pure, divine truth above the pains of the world. I knew the sting of rejection. I knew how loneliness bored into your chest and didn't leave.

I was born of scripture and devotion so intricate, someone—some soul of extraordinary faith—must have spent years weaving verse into flesh. There had to be meaning behind such creation. *Why bring something so deliberate into being, then leave it untethered?* I needed a solution to that question.

If I could find the one who wrote me, or at least learn *why*, I might finally stop chasing a shape that never fit. Might stop trying to cram myself into the hollow mold others left behind.

If I'd ever been sacred, the feeling hadn't followed me.

I wasn't the angel the old Tormites made me out to be. I also wasn't the monster the people of Rarek made me now.

But I believed in justice, truth, right and wrong, self-determination. The faith. Its weight carved into my chest.

I didn't want to be worshiped. I didn't want to be feared. I just wanted to *be*. But the world never let me.

So I kept moving forward. Kept chasing the answers. Sometimes I didn't know where I was going—but I knew standing still had never made the shouting stop.

8 - City Under Siege

I approached Rarek beneath its silent stone walls as clouds darkened the sky. The western gate stood wide, yawning like a showpiece—robust sills and heavy lintels carved with lion heads, yet worn smooth by centuries of open invitation. A fortress that had never needed to lock its doors.

From the road, Rarek looked unchanged. Still a bulwark pretending it had something worth defending. But the closer I got, the more that illusion frayed.

The color had drained from the stones. The streets were still. No scent of fresh-baked bread—just soot, rust, and that ever-present trace of rat poison.

This was the real Rarek. Not its celebration farce, but its *everyday* face. Pale and worn. Self-important and sour. A city of old grudges and newer cruelties it hadn't yet learned to name.

The gates let me in, as they always did. But that wasn't welcome. That was indifference. It wasn't Remembrance anymore. No one had an excuse to act kind.

As if on cue, a teenage boy stepped out of a cart's shadow and spat in my face. I flinched before wiping the moisture from my cheek. His eyes were hard, angry, full of something I didn't recognize. He said, loud enough for half the street to hear: "Filthy glyph-bearer."

"Excuse me?" I asked, tone as measured as I could make it. I'd weathered insults before, but this one felt different.

"You glow-people... siphoning wealth for your miracles, bleeding us poor to enrich your relics," he sneered. "The new tax is the reason we're all going hungry!" With that he turned on his heel and stomped off. A few others gave wary, yet eager nods of agreement. None met my eyes.

I stood frozen, confused. Ethereals had been the subject of distrust and suspicion for years, but never outright violence. My sisters and I had absorbed stares, avoided gatherings, walked carefully... but this? This was new.

New tax? Famine? The boy spoke as if I had personally drained the lifeblood from the city while lining my own pockets. I looked around at the people on the street, avoiding my gaze and going about their business. None of them looked any thinner. I shook my head, pressing fingers to the spot he'd spat. His revulsion had weight, fear made physical. Wherever it came from, this boy had believed the lie—accepted this false cause.

I took a steadying breath and moved on. A poison had spread. I didn't know how deep it ran yet, but with every step, the city's walls felt narrower, the welcome colder.

Dread stirred in the pit of my chest. And I wondered: how long until that spit became something solid? A rock, a fist, a blade?

I didn't have the luxury to ponder. For I heard that terrible soothing voice again, addressing the people.

Aurelian Vale.

He stood on the low balcony above the market entrance, draped in plain, sturdy wool that made him look like a neighbor, not a leader. Behind him hung banners emblazoned with some new sigil. Not the city seal, nor the royal family's crest, not even the chapel's symbol. It was also featured on his clothing. *His* brand.

Below, a throng gathered, faces flicking between anger and longing. I kept my distance, heart tightening.

He spoke with the honeyed tenor of someone who'd already given them relief.

"Friends, I hear your struggles. I feel your hunger. That new levy isn't a burden—it's a yoke. A yoke worn by honest folk, starving so that relics and rituals get their gold."

He paused, eyes sweeping the crowd with synthetic warmth.

"The King has been told. But he supports those… traditionalists—those Torm worshipers that preach self-sacrifice while their priests feast at our expense."

A ripple of agreement passed through the crowd. They weren't shocked; they were certain, and desperate. He had them.

He reached beneath his simple tunic and pulled out a handful of coins. "These came from your coin purses—levied under the guise of supporting the chapel, but I haven't seen a single candle lit in that place since Remembrance. Not one word of your grievances has been heard."

"Miracles?" Vale scoffed, letting the word hang bitter on his tongue. "You pay for relics that don't heal. Prayers that don't end hunger. Traditions that offer no return. Yet your burden grows heavier."

He held the coins aloft. "Let me be clear with you, good citizens—this tax, this so-called levy? I am the one collecting it. That much is true. I carry it on behalf of the King, who has been... persuaded by the same false creed that left our city to rot while old shrines are maintained and restored."

A few murmurs rose.

"Tormites preach sacrifice. And the King?" Vale spread his arms in mock humility. "He believes it. He thinks you should go without. That you should suffer nobly for some long-dead god who mistook misery for virtue."

A gasp from the crowd. A cry of "Shame!"

He held up a small, empty chest.

"Money talks where faith stammers. If the crown won't heed your hunger, we'll buy its ear. I must collect this tithe, but I won't deliver it to the palace. Not yet. Not until the King hears you. Not until he sees what his people truly need."

Vale's voice grew sharper, more intimate, like a father disappointed on their behalf. He drew his hand into a fist.

"I know you. You want your children fed. You want your shops open. You want laughter and warmth, not the cold martyrdom these relic-worshipers demand."

The crowd roared approval, whipped into allegiance. The slur from earlier rang louder now in retrospect, more than insult—it was creed. I watched them cling to his cadence, nodding, clapping, believing. This was no sermon, this was a contract signed in the air.

I stood, rooted and furious. He was using their needs as bait, twisting their worry into weaponized loyalty. He gave them a villain—and painted me and my sisters into it. And somewhere behind that applause, I heard my faith being unmade.

Vale stepped off the balcony and disappeared into the swarm, his banners trailing behind him. The crowd followed, hungry not for salvation, but for anything that promised relief. A chorus of clinks and jingles joined the uproar as people opened their purses and handed over even more of their supposedly-insufficient earnings.

I remained behind, my chest tightening like a bundle of cords. Their acceptance of his lies had gone deeper than I'd imagined. As I watched the last ripple of the crowd fade around the corner, I realized this harvest he was reaping would take far more than words to undo. And my light dimmed slightly. Enough to remind me of how much was already at stake.

I wanted to step forward. To climb that stage, wrench the truth out of Vale's mouth with words or fists, and drag his lies into the open. But the crowd, hungry for blood, would never hear me. Not like this. Not now.

They cheered him as if he were the god they'd once feared.

Wasn't Kirtana supposed to speak with him? Wasn't she going to temper this madness before it spread? She was never naïve. She knew the danger of letting a charming tongue wag unchecked. What happened?

I turned, fists clenched, heat boiling just under my skin despite the chill in the air. I had to find her.

Something had gone wrong.

The chapel looked tired.

Numerous new cracks traced the stained glass like veins, its muted colors further dulled beneath a film of dust. Dirt was everywhere; the entire structure looked like it had been haphazardly painted in brown. Several new chips marred the stone walls, doorframes, and steps. Even without Kirtana's meticulous maintenance, time didn't move this fast. This damage wasn't from weather or age. This was something else. Something unnatural.

I stepped inside, and the air met me like a held breath. Cold. Stale.

Kirtana looked up from the altar, eyes wide. "Daelon?"

She crossed the nave in hurried steps, too fast for someone who always moved with intention. She reached for my arms, then hesitated, curling her fingers back to her chest. There was a tremor in her too taut voice.

"He's turning them against us," she said. "And I can't stop it."

She wasn't weeping. But her calm had slipped its leash. Her face, always a still pond, now showed ripples, waves along the edges of composure. Fear made her voice thin. Desperation sat in her posture, head low, shoulders raised like she expected the roof to come down next.

I'd seen this fraying sanity before. Eryndra, at the fountain, fists clenched and jaw locked. That was her version of fear. This... this was Kirtana's. This was the sound of something sacred coming undone.

"His poison is spreading, Daelon. Even the King's being painted as a tyrant, corrupt... a sympathizer to our cause."

"For what?" I said. "What power does the King even *have*? He didn't even show his face at Remembrance. He hasn't issued a decree in months. He's a statue with a signature."

Kirtana's expression darkened. "And yet, they're blaming him. They think he's sheltering us. That he's keeping the Tormites comfortable while they starve."

I stiffened. "Are they starving?"

"No," she said, shaking her head. "There's no famine. No theft. The chapel hasn't received any new requests for aid. No new taxes. No ration order. If anything, the nobles are spending *more*, to keep up appearances. Nothing's changed. Except what they *believe*."

"So it's a story," I exhaled through my teeth. "He's not reporting decay, he's manufacturing it. We're just a new enemy they can point to and say, 'You're why things feel wrong'."

I rubbed my jaw. "How is he getting away with it? They're not stupid, Kirtana. They've lived through lean years. They know what real suffering looks like."

"They're tired," she said softly. "And scared. People have started whispering that the King's too passive. That he's letting us rebuild too much power."

"But we never had power." My voice was raw with disbelief. "Tormism was never the law. Never the treasury. We were servants of sacrifice, not rulers."

She met my gaze. "Not anymore. They don't remember what we were. Vale's rewritten the story—and handed them someone to blame for how they feel."

"They feel *aimless*," I said bitterly. "They're *bored.* And instead of asking why their joy is hollow, why the festivals don't fill them, they blame the ones who still live by something deeper. Something harder."

I turned and paced for a moment.

"This doesn't make any sense," I said. "Last I was here, Vale was *preaching* Torm. Now he's demonizing us. What's his motive?"

Kirtana's face crumpled up like a paper ball. "I don't know. He claims he works *for* the King while denouncing him in the same breath. Says he serves the people but lies to them, stokes their fear and rage. He clearly has sway, Daelon, and no one's stopping him. But if he's already this powerful, what more could he want?"

I said nothing. I thought of the chest; the coins. The way he'd called them to action not with weapons, but with donations. I had a suspicion. But this couldn't *just* be about gold. Could it?

He was extravagantly well-dressed when I'd first seen him. Well-spoken and knowledgeable. Youthful, attractive. That polished confidence that didn't come from arrogance, but certainty. Assertive in a way that disarmed you. He claimed to be a scholar of Talakit: a land whose universities demanded generational wealth just to walk their halls. If that was true, if he really came from that background... he couldn't possibly *need* money.

Why come to a poorer kingdom just to bleed its people dry? Why risk the attention of a royal court if all he wanted was coin?

There had to be something else. Some other reason to relocate, here of all places. To turn the people of Rarek into angry, faithful pawns. To stoke them like embers and let them burn their own homes from the inside. What *was* he playing at?

I glanced past her toward the shrine. Empty.

"Where is Eryndra?"

Kirtana exhaled a sharp, weary breath. "Up at the palace. With the guard."

Of course she was.

"She's convinced it's the only place she can be of use," Kirtana said. "But her association with the King doesn't help—it only confirms people's worst suspicions."

I opened my mouth, but she shook her head.

"She won't stop. She thinks their unrest proves she's right to be there. That the city needs guarding from itself. That her post is proof of our legitimacy." Her tone twisted into something bitter. "But the more she shows up in plate and sigil, the more they hate us."

I looked around the chapel. The marks, the dust, the splintered edges.

"They've started throwing dirt when they pass," she said, quiet. "Stones, too, when no one's watching. And without Eryndra here to answer them, they get bolder. I sweep it away, patch what I can, but..."

She didn't finish the sentence.

I felt her withering next to me, her strength buckling under the weight of resignation. Her fingers twisted absently in her wrappings—something she did only when deeply unsettled. So I tried to pull her mind away, if only for a moment.

"Have you seen or heard anything about Luna?"

Her sigh was immediate and bitter, and I knew I'd failed. "Daelon, I haven't had the worry to spare for a lost child. Not with everything else…" Her voice caught, but she steadied it, forcing herself upright again. "No. We haven't heard a word. Eryndra's been keeping her ear to the guard, even the palace. If someone had seen her—especially someone like her—word would've gotten around. You know how the nobles talk. They can't keep quiet about a new soup, let alone a new race."

I nodded slowly, eyes falling to the dusty stone at my feet. A child who could walk through walls, silent and small. She could be anywhere, or nowhere. I hated the thought of her surviving alone out there, in a city that had grown cold to even those who lit its streets.

But before I could dwell too long, Kirtana shifted. Not out of comfort, but perhaps out of concern. Or guilt.

"What about your latest search?" she asked gently. "Did you find what you were looking for?"

The chill came back. That mountain and its ever-watching cold. Its silence. Its cruelty. I remembered the brittle sound of my knuckles breaking that altar, the ugliness of my own rage painted across another god's shrine. I remembered the light dimming, the fire of shame flaring and then dying to coals.

I didn't answer. I just shook my head.

Kirtana's expression softened. "I'm sorry," she murmured. "That it… didn't go as you'd hoped."

I nodded, barely.

She glanced to the window, the cracks letting in dull, crooked light. "Has Stetson found any new leads?"

I exhaled slowly. "I haven't been back to the library yet."

Her brow furrowed—just slightly, but for Kirtana, that was a shout. "You should go," she said. "See if he's turned up anything. He always digs up something."

I looked around the chapel, its stone more weathered than it should've been, windows spidered with hairline fractures. The air was still.

Too still.

"You haven't been singing," I said quietly. "Have you?"

Kirtana looked away.

"Why?" I asked. "It always lightens your spirit. And theirs. Especially during the leaner seasons."

She hesitated, then sighed. "I tried. A few times."

Her voice dipped.

"They shouted. Said I was making a mockery of their hunger. Of their grief. That joy—*faith*—was insulting while they suffered."

Her hand brushed the hem of her sleeve. "Once, they threw stones their at *me*, instead of the chapel."

I flinched.

"But you know me," she said, with a faint, crooked smile. "Once I start a song, I have to finish it."

Her voice trembled.

"I've taken a few bruises. Nothing serious. But... I haven't sung much since. I'm afraid of what might come next."

I stepped closer, eyes lifting her hand and touching the linen wrap around her wrist. A line of script peeked through the folds.

"*Make a joyful noise unto the stars,*" I murmured, tracing the verse with my finger, "*that they might remember we were here.*"

She smiled, softer this time. A fragile warmth behind the weariness.

"Staying silent while voices of deceit grow louder doesn't give the people anything to choose from," I said. "You should remind them there's another way. That his voice isn't the only one. This city has forgotten so much. Let them remember beauty. Let them remember *you*."

She didn't speak, not right away. Then, a quiet, unconvincing, "I'll try. Now please, go see Stetson."

I slipped out from the chapel, taking the long way through back lanes and quieter alleys, steering clear of clusters that looked too opinionated. Couldn't be too subtle though; skulking looked suspicious. The guards still held their posts, slack in their helmets, chatting idly as if nothing had changed. Vale hadn't gotten to them yet, it seemed. Small blessings.

The library wasn't far, but every footstep sounded louder now, each step an announcement. I kept my head low.

Inside, the air greeted me like a sealed tomb, thick and stale, as though no one had opened the door since I left. Books lined the shelves, untouched, gathering not just dust but irrelevance. The floor looked like it had never once seen a broom, my footprints the only signs of recent life.

Where were people getting their information from? If not here, surely not anywhere it could be trusted. Perhaps if they thought to set foot in this place, they'd be more equipped to see through Aurelian Vale's lies. I shoved that thought aside and scanned for the broad figure of Stetson.

He wasn't at the front desk: his favorite snoozing spot. I walked to the back to look for him.

As I rounded the corner between shelves, something blurred toward my face. I jerked my head back, and the object halted mere inches away. I blinked, saw it was a heavy chair leg.

"By Tyr's mercy—" Stetson gasped, startling himself almost as much as me.

He stumbled forward, half-apologizing, one hand wrapped around the blunt wood. "Daelon! Forgive me—foolish, inattentive old bones. Why didn't you announce yourself?" His voice shook between relief and irritation.

"I could ask *you* the same thing," I said, jaw tight, taking a half-step back from his makeshift weapon. "Have you taken leave of your senses? Posting yourself up between the stacks like a night-watchman to ambush visitors? Is this why no one's been here?"

He sighed, a deep, rattling sound that seemed to settle dust from the rafters. "Oh, they've been coming in, alright. Not for reading, though." He gestured with the chair leg toward a darkened scorch mark near one of the carpets. "Tried to burn a few volumes last week. Caught two of them with a flask and matches."

I turned my eyes toward the mark, the edge of it still curled like charred parchment. "I wager someone's gone and told them that these books are where all their troubles began."

He nodded and muttered something obscene under his breath. "Easier to believe that than to read, I suppose. That boy from Talakit's got everyone convinced that print is the devil."

I took a closer look at him. Bruises on his face and arms. Cuts on his hands. Hair a frazzled mess. Bloodshot eyes.

"I've been yelled at, pushed, nearly clobbered," he said. Then he tapped the chair leg against the stone. "So I try to stay out of sight. Catch 'em by surprise and run 'em off."

I narrowed my gaze, back teeth grinding together. "The guards haven't done anything about it?"

"The guards?" he asked, the sarcasm dry as old vellum. "They're *ever so busy*, don't you know? All that *nothing* they've got to get done. Hardly enough hours in the day to see to it all. Can't even be bothered to keep the market square from turning into a brawl some days."

He sighed and tapped the chair leg on his own before finishing. "But enough about that. I think I have something worth your time."

He led me back up toward the front, his steps slower than usual. His fingers tapped absently at the surface, like a preacher drumming up courage before a sermon.

"Well," he said, dragging the word out, "Bad news first: still no confirmation on that shrine in no-man's land. No name, no symbol, no exact location. Whoever built it didn't leave much of a footprint. Still digging."

I nodded, already expecting as much. "And the good news?"

Stetson's grin was almost sheepish. "I, ah… may have been investing a little scholarly effort elsewhere. You know. In the city. Among the elven community."

I raised a brow.

"Quality time," he said, winking, "with some of our more *graceful* residents."

He waited for me to sigh. I didn't.

"Anyway," he continued, clearing his throat, "I slipped a few questions into the pillow talk. Silverstrand Enclave—name rang no bells. But when I described what you'd told me… the sideways waterfalls, the biting flowers, the real sky... several of them mentioned old stories. Fairytales, really. Children's fancies."

The sag of my shoulders must have shown through the wrappings, because he lifted a hand.

"Now, now. Don't write it off yet," he said quickly. "You know how elves are. They love their secrets. And they keep them *very* well. But if you—" he made a crude gesture with his hips, "—you can get them talking. Loosen the tongue, so to speak."

I stared. He moved on.

"Turns out, most of the elven lineages do have enclaves. Remote, hidden places, often built where they don't need defending because no one knows they exist. One group, bit of a whispered legend even among other elves, are said to have purple skin, and the ability to walk through walls. Apparently they live behind some kind of 'veil'. Not a metaphorical one. A real thing. Maybe invisible. Maybe solid. Depends on who's telling it. Some think you have to have their phasing ability to get through the veil, others swear that there have been visitors allowed into the enclave."

It fit her. Too perfectly. The slivered details he gave: purple skin, phasing, the veil.

Luna had never told me how she was separated from her family. Not in words. But if she didn't know how to find her way back, then it made sense. She'd been exiled by ignorance. A child stuck in a world of strangers because the door home was lost to her.

I leaned forward. "Did any of them say where this veil might be?"

Stetson grinned, one eye squinting shut as he tapped a thick finger to his temple. "None of them had the full map," he said. "But they dropped crumbs. Moon angles, mountain lines, river mouths. Classic fae stuff. Riddles wrapped in poetry."

He ducked down beneath the counter, and I heard the unmistakable rustle of parchment on parchment, tomes knocking against each other. He emerged with an armful of chaos. Scrolls half-curled, notes scribbled on repurposed ledger paper, full spines of books cracked with age and use.

"And you know me," he said with a grin, sweeping the mess out across the counter. "Can't resist a good riddle."

I watched as Stetson's mania rolled out across the counter like a flood. Vellum layers peeled and stacked, their edges curling and trembling under the weight of frantic explanations. Sheets of parchment with more arrows than words, crossing themselves out and redrawn again in careless ink. His compass, worn to near rust, swept in circles as if it too sought something just beyond the page. He narrated his process in half-sentences, sometimes to me, sometimes to himself, holding papers to the light, cross-referencing ridges with verses from children's tales like they were divine law.

It was clear he'd been busy with more than just the ladies and hiding between the shelves these last few months. Perhaps he needed this to distract him from the possibility of folks burning the entire building down.

When he finally exhaled and leaned back, hands planted on his hips like he'd just rerouted a river, he turned his head to me and beamed with triumph.

I stared at him, numb. Like a child left behind in a mathematics lecture where all the variables were named after birds.

"So... do you know where it is?" I asked.

His grin drooped. "You didn't hear a word I said, did you?"

I said nothing.

With a dramatic sigh and a theatrical roll of his eyes, he tapped one of the six maps. A modest circle, drawn in faint charcoal, sat quietly amid the chaos.

"There," he said. "Right there. That's where I think it is."

His confidence had returned, but it wore a caveat now. Something quieter, more brittle.

"What I don't know," he added, "is *when* it's there. Or how to get in."

"'*When*' it's there?" I echoed.

"You heard right," Stetson confirmed, his voice slipping back into lecture mode, though this time with less haste. "I can decrypt their poetry and fluff about our world well enough, but their magic?" He gave a soft scoff, waving a hand over the scattered pages. "I haven't got a lick of it myself. Can't even charm a flame, much less make a passageway vanish."

He gestured to a set of verses near the margin of one parchment, tapping one finger along its cursive twists. "Best I can tell, it's fixed in location, but it doesn't always… *work*. Seems to go dormant. Or disappears. Or maybe just won't let you in unless the conditions are right. Could be time of day. Could be a season. Hell, might even be emotional. Elven magic is dramatic like that."

He rubbed at his temple, squinting. "What's worse, it says only people the elves *want* in can pass through. Which, sure, makes sense if you're inside—but what if you're outside? What if some poor bastard *wants in,* and someone on the other side *doesn't* want them? Does the veil listen to the outsider's will? Or the insider's rejection?" His shrug was heavy, frustrated.

That thought clung to me, wrapping its icy fingers around my ribs and pulling. What if Luna *did* know where the veil was? What if she'd stood before it, fingers outstretched, whispering pleas into air that didn't answer?

She had said she had a family. Said it in the way children do: confident, absolute, with no space for doubt. They still lived there: behind the veil.

So how had she ended up outside? Had she wandered too far? Slipped out during the wrong hour, and the doorway simply... stopped existing?

My chest constricted, breath thin and ragged despite the calm around me. I remembered the alley. The stone I'd knocked on. The silence I'd left her in. And her voice, cracked and trembling, echoed again in my skull:

"I wanna go home..."

The stabbing pain in my heart froze and forced the fissure in my chest wider.

She didn't ask for comfort. She didn't ask for protection. She asked for belonging. For the right to stand among her own again.

That right had been stolen from her.

Luna was gentle. Open-hearted. Even after everything they'd done to her, there was still brightness in her. An innocent zest for life.

She was only a child. A girl too young to know what ideology even meant. And yet they'd branded her.

I still didn't know why. What fear could she have possibly inspired? What prophecy or superstition could ever make adults lift a heated iron toward a child? Whatever story they told themselves, it *couldn't* be justified.

A child's back should never carry proof of an adult's cowardice.

I'd seen the familiar look of discomfort in the faces around her. As if her presence disrupted the stories they wanted to tell themselves. As if by existing, she reminded them of the gaps in their worldview.

The same looks I was given in Rarek. The same cold glances and narrowed eyes. The same uneasy shifting when I walked too close. I knew what it was to be a symbol others rejected. To walk through a city that once made space for you—and now flinched like you were a mirror they'd rather break than face.

But Luna's pain wasn't abstract. It wasn't centuries of cultural drift or decades of spiritual amnesia. It was now. More importantly, it was solvable.

And I needed that.

I needed something I could put my hands around. Something I could fix, or fight for. Something that hadn't already slipped through my fingers like every other sacred thing.

I regained my footing when Stetson's voice broke through the growing ache.

"How did you learn about this place?" he asked. "It's quite a well-kept secret, even amongst the elves."

I told him how I'd met her: the carriage driver's tremulous description of finding Luna, small and shivering under a tree, rocking back and forth and sobbing. She didn't know where she was, or how she'd come to be alone in the wilderness. He'd scoured the area around their path—for hours—looking for signs of a village, a road, anything. Finding nothing, he coaxed her onto the wagon. Shared his food. Only when her trembling slowed did she agree to let him bring her to Rarek.

Stetson listened, silent. As I finished, the gravity of it finally sunk into his bones. "So… she might still be trying," he said softly. "To get back."

I nodded, but words failed me. Instead, I clenched my hands and stared at the maps and riddles sprawled before us. Even if I went to the location Stetson had shown me, I had no presumption they would let me in. Or hear me out. Not without Luna in tow. What kind of enclave answers the door to a stranger and a prayer? I wanted desperately to help, but I would have to find her first.

How does one hunt a ghost?

I turned back to him, gave him my thanks. Told him to stay safe. He nodded, a worn look softening his expression for just a moment, and rapped his knuckles against the broken chair leg like it was a warding talisman. "You might need to consider arming yourself as well, especially given the circumstances."

He knew my opinion. He knew it well. Owning a weapon invites one to use it. Even when the situation doesn't call for one. It sends a message: escalation, not understanding. And I had learned, in more ways than one, that nothing provokes suspicion faster than preparation. The last thing I needed to do in a city teetering toward hostility was to signal that I might deserve it.

I didn't respond in words. Just a breath through my nose and a slow humph, enough to remind him what I thought of blades and bludgeons. He didn't press it.

And I left. The door creaked behind me, then sealed with the usual sigh of dust and age.

The sky had gone red. That bruised kind of red that turns shadows to accusations. Evening had laid its fingers on Rarek. Luckily, there was no sign of Vale or his whipped-up mob. Here, for now, the streets were quiet. Wary quiet, not peaceful, like a house where shouting had just ceased.

I kept my head down and my pace steady as I walked toward the chapel, letting my thoughts wander somewhere safer. If Luna was still in Rarek, there had to be something that could draw her out. Some flicker of memory or joy strong enough to coax her from wherever she was hiding.

She'd liked Remembrance, hadn't she? She had seemed to enjoy the festival's noise, the food, the dancing... though never for long. She darted from one delight to the next like a sparrow amidst breadcrumbs. But there was one thing that had held her. One thing that had made her stop. Kirtana's voice.

That moment came back to me in full color. Her breath caught, her hands still for the first time, eyes wide and brimming not with fear, but something softer. She had stood rooted, caught in the current of that solemn, requious melody. Kirtana's songs weren't just beautiful, they were safe. And Luna, more than anything, had needed that. As I walked, I could swear I heard it.

I *had* heard it. Not memory. Not a trick of the mind. Faint but unmistakable, the rise and fall of Kirtana's voice weaving through the brick and dust of Rarek. She was singing.

I picked up my pace.

9 - The Last Refrain

A few paces from the courtyard's turn, I heard the difference.

Kirtana's voice was still there, steady and clear, but something pressed against it. Male voices. Not singing. The sound was low, guttural, slurred by disdain. They weren't shouting, not quite. But they weren't just talking, either. The tone was mocking. Needling. Cruel in the way only those sure of their numbers dared to be.

I quickened again, trying to parse the words as I approached.

"Save it, witch. Ain't no meals in your melody."

"She sings, we starve. Maybe she likes it that way."

"What's she even praising? Their god's already dead."

"Must be summoning another famine, right?"

Tight and ugly laughter spilled over the end of that last jab. My stomach knotted. These weren't idle insults. They were bludgeons, swung with the confidence of a crowd.

I rounded the corner.

A group of eight men had her surrounded. Kirtana stood at the edge of the chapel's crumbling steps, wrapped in radiant gold, her palms pressed together before her chest. Her posture was composed but taut, a reed not yet bent by the wind. A glow pulsed from above her chin; her mouth still moved; the notes still came. But her gaze flicked over the men now and then, measuring distance, bracing.

None of the men carried weapons. They didn't need to. Their posture was its own kind of blade: chests puffed, feet spaced wide, limbs twitching like horses before a break. They should've been softened by the song. They weren't.

And still she sang. I'd never known her to end a song early. She'd once spellbound a man so completely he tripped over his own feet, cracking his head on the cobbles. She kept singing while cradling the bleeding man. She'd finished the entire hymn while helping to treat his wounds. This was nothing. And yet...

I could see the edge of fear in her. Not for herself. But for what they might do to the chapel. To the ideals it represented.

My stride faltered. The weight of her song settled on me like mist—thick, clinging, gentle. Too gentle. I didn't stop entirely, but each step after was harder to place. Her voice pulled the ire from the air, dulled it into something softer. But it also pulled at me. Eased the spine from my resolve.

That was the cruelty of it. Kirtana's voice could hush rage, lull sorrow, still the blood in your veins... but it left no room for fire. No room for interruption, for action. For years I'd thought it a holy thing. Now, I wasn't sure if it was grace or paralysis.

I clenched my fists at my sides. Tried to speak. The words crumbled behind my teeth. I could barely summon my own voice, let alone the tone I'd need to break a crowd like this. To make them see me. Feel me. Kirtana's notes made confrontation feel like desecration. Like yelling in a cathedral.

Only Eryndra ever managed to bark orders through Kirtana's melodies. Somehow, her fury could weave through the hymn without shattering it. I never could.

And Kirtana... she wouldn't stop. Not for her safety, not for mine. Not even for the stone beneath her feet. She wouldn't end a song before it was meant to end. That was her oath. Her stubbornness. Her burden.

So I stood there, half-lost in the lull, too stunned to act, watching a group of jackals gather teeth.

The tiniest twitch of movement. A speck of color. Something that didn't belong to the drab cobbles or the soot-dark walls or the faces curled into masks of contempt. It tugged at the edge of my vision.

I managed to wrench my gaze away from Kirtana and turned. And there she was.

Luna.

Just as she had been during Remembrance: still, small, carved from the breath between two notes. Her eyes wide, her lips parted in wonder. The light touched her hair in patches, dirty and matted though it was, and for a moment she looked less like a child and more like some feral sylph pulled from the pages of a forgotten tale.

She'd thinned. Gods, she'd thinned. A skeleton wearing a child's costume. Her elbows knifed beneath the skin, her cheekbones protruding as if they would breach the lilac surface. How she stood upright I couldn't say. I'd seen canvas with more slack in it.

I wanted to move. Wanted to close the distance between us, wrap her in what little warmth I had left and whisper the lies every child deserved to hear: that she was safe, that everything was going to be okay.

But I couldn't. And she wasn't. And it wasn't.

The men finally moved. It started with a lurch, like the breaking of a wave. Two of them stepped in, hands clawing at Kirtana's shawl, her arms, snatching at the trailing threads of her bindings. Others followed, emboldened, forming a cruel rhythm of jerking motions and shouted slurs. Kirtana staggered under their touch, her voice skipping like a broken wagon wheel, catching as fists met ribs, as palms shoved her shoulders.

But she didn't stop.

Even as they struck her, her voice rose again. Shaky now, brittle as winter glass, but carrying that same mournful clarity. A hymn not for them, but for anyone who might remember what it meant to weep for something sacred. She was singing not to soothe them, not to halt their violence, but to be heard. To be seen. To remain.

Each gasp between the notes carved space into the air where my feet could move. One step. Then another. My limbs felt sludged, as though wrapped in tar, but I advanced, pulled not by courage but obligation. Their eyes weren't on me. Or they didn't care. Why would they? I was just another statue on a dying god's lawn.

I couldn't shout. Couldn't summon the voice that had defused mobs and calmed armies.

All I could do was watch.

Across the courtyard from me, Luna still stood. Her face was changing, something like worry pooling behind the enchantment, but her body remained rigid, transfixed. She too was trapped beneath Kirtana's song. It held us both hostage.

But Kirtana kept singing.

"I know what'll shut her up."

The voice pierced through the song, leering and mean, as one of the men fumbled beneath his coat. I saw the glint before the shape: a knife, small and jagged, but more than enough.

Kirtana's tone wavered. She tried to pull away, to make a break for the chapel door like it could shelter her voice... but still singing. They grabbed her wrists, her ankles, forced her down onto the stone steps with a thud that stole half the note from her mouth. She writhed under them, but the hymn threaded on.

The knife-wielder climbed atop her, one knee pressed into her ribs, the other braced to keep balance. He yanked her head back by the wrappings, exposing her throat like he was about to pour her voice out onto the ground. She kept singing. Even as her spine arched unnaturally beneath him, even as she gasped between verses—still, she sang.

I was only steps away, but it felt like miles. I moved like the world was tilted, slow and sticky, wading through the bog of helplessness. I opened my mouth, but nothing emerged. Not even a whisper.

Then came the break.

A wet sound gurgled up from her throat. And the music stopped.

The moment her song fell silent, it was as if the world gave me back to myself. The momentum of those twelve lethargic steps may as well have been a hundred. I crashed into them like a boulder down a hill. The men scattered, some tripping, others buckling beneath me as I hurled myself into the fray. I seized the knife-wielder by the nape of his neck. His limbs flailed, too slow, too late, and I drove his skull into the stone arch of the chapel door. The impact shuddered, sick and final, but I heard no sound. He slumped. Unconscious, or dead? I hadn't the time or the care to check.

I turned on the others. One still on the stairs was scrambling to rise. I kicked him square in the face, sent him sprawling down to the dirt where even grace wouldn't stoop to lift him.

The rest hesitated. They saw me now. Their eyes went wide. One of them began to raise his hands, a placating gesture that shook at the elbows. Too late.

Before I could advance, a gasp cut through the tension. I turned just in time to see a flash of purple and green—Luna. She pivoted, light as air, and slipped into the chapel wall like fog through a grate, vanishing into the stone as though she'd never been real.

My voice finally returned to me, and I intended to rally the city.

"GUARDS!"

The word echoed louder than it should have, as if Rarek itself had been holding its breath. I felt it rattle and bounce off the stone walls, but the silence still filled my ears. It must have rang true. The men broke. What courage they'd borrowed from each other drained in a heartbeat, and they scattered like roaches when the torchlight hits.

I stomped forward—one pace only—prepared to chase them down, to drag them back, to supplant justice with wrath.

A tiny splash, barely audible, heard louder than any crashing thunder, as my hearing also returned to me. A warm, wet sensation seeped across my foot.

I looked down. Her blood had soaked through the cloth of my bindings. It was spreading, blooming red against my script-wrapped skin.

Kirtana.

My anger swept away like dust upon the wind. I dropped to my knees, the stone biting into them unnoticed beneath the weight of it all. Kirtana writhed, one hand clutched to her throat, trying in vain to press the blood back in. It slipped through her fingers, soaking the wrappings on her arms, staining scripture until it ran unreadable. My eyes caught on a phrase, just as the blood dashed away the last of its legibility.

"Make a joyful noise unto the stars, that they might remember we were here."

It split me open. She was still trying. The gurgling came again—rhythmic in time. A desperate attempt to finish what she had begun. To honor the music, even as it betrayed her. Tears traced down her cheeks, not for the pain, but for the verses unfinished. She mourned not herself, but the silence. That heretical absence where a song should have been.

Her light flickered. Dimmed by despair and exertion, by the furious devotion of a soul unwilling to let go. It faltered in rhythm with her pulse, dipping and flaring, a candle protesting a storm. Her face shone with fear—for faltering, for needing help, for not finishing.

Even as the sky bled above her, even as the warmth left her hands, she burned.

I tore the wrappings from my arms. They came undone in a flurry, scripture snapping free from skin like banners ripped in wind. Light flared from my exposed limbs—a blaze, a furious radience spilling into every corner of the courtyard. I wanted to drown out the world. To cast the red from the sky, to undo the stain that spread across the stone.

I pressed my hands to her neck, her blood slick against my palms, and wrapped my own verse around her throat. The ink smeared—"endure" bleeding into "faith" into nothing—but I pulled tight. Tight enough to seal the wound, to keep what was left of her inside.

She didn't need breath. None of us did. But the voice came from someplace deeper. A place neither light nor scripture could reach. Still she tried to sing, and still I held the torn shreds of my own story to her skin, as if my words could make her whole.

My light grew. So fierce it bleached the stone, seared tears from my cheeks before they could fall. I couldn't see my hands anymore, or the blood beneath them. I couldn't see her face, only the faint flicker still pulsing beneath her skin. She was still holding on.

So I held tighter.

A clatter of metal on stone broke the silence behind me.

Armor scraped, boots skidded, then a sharp gasp as the newcomer staggered beneath the weight of my light. I couldn't see him, not through the brilliance I refused to dim, but I heard the shuffle of his pauldron as he raised a hand to shield his eyes.

"By the crown, what's going on here?" he stammered.

"Eryndra!" My voice cracked like a whip. "Bring Eryndra Caelux here, now!"

"What?"

I didn't soften. "Eryndra! Now!"

There was a beat of stunned silence, then the click of heels pivoting and the hurried cadence of departure. He was one of the good ones, the rare few who obeyed orders first and asked questions later. But still, his footfalls were too slow. Everything was too slow.

I turned back to Kirtana, whose fingers gripped my wrists now with failing strength, her body trembling against the force of my light.

"I'm sorry," I whispered. "I asked you to sing."

Her grip tightened for a second. Then loosened.

Agonizing minutes pressed by. I could feel it the moment it stopped: the faint, desperate rhythm she'd been keeping time with beneath my hands. The blood no longer spilled between my fingers. Her limbs, once locked in stubborn fight, fell slack.

This was the end, I thought.

I eased back the light, dreading what I'd see. Preparing myself for the dull, cold ruin of a life extinguished. For a body wrapped in scripture with no voice left to read it. For a dark, lightless husk.

But I was wrong. What I saw was worse.

She was still there. Alive, if the word had any meaning, but the gold was gone. Her light, once warm and unwavering, had turned a mournful teal. Not extinguished. Not destroyed.

My sister had hollowed.

When movement returned to me—numb, reluctant, bitter—I gathered her in my arms. My sister. Or whatever remained of her. Her light did not protest. Her limbs did not flinch. Her voice, once the axis around which the room turned, was still.

I stepped over the man who had done this. His body lay twisted and broken, head blooming red against the chapel steps. I did not check for breath.

Inside, the chapel had never felt more empty. Its silence was not peace but absence. Each echo of my footsteps was a dirge. I carried her up the aisle and laid her on the table before the shrine, as if placing her on a pyre, though there was no fire hot enough to cleanse this.

And I prayed.

Not because I believed it would help. Not because I thought He still listened. But because I had nothing left. I prayed; not for justice or retribution, but for mercy.

"Torm: right hand of Tyr, patron of duty and sacrifice... spare her this fate. Give her back her light. Our numbers are too few to afford her silence. And I... I could not bear a world without her song."

No answer.

The stillness fractured—not by a powerful, disembodied voice and a thunder of divinity, but by the pitter-patter of bare feet and naivety. I didn't turn. I didn't need to. The air itself told me: innocent, tentative, drawn forward by curiosity that just barely outweighed fear. Luna had crept out from the place where she'd folded herself into the chapel wall, her silhouette flickering in the edge of my vision.

"Is… is she okay?" she asked, voice small and brittle. "Why is she blue?"

I couldn't answer her. I couldn't even look at her.

I wept. I tried to silence it with a fist to my mouth, but my shoulders betrayed me, trembling in great waves, as I choked and gasped and heaved on sobs.

How could I explain to a child that someone had kept singing as the world tore itself apart around her?

How could I explain that the blue meant the world had won?

She shuffled closer. Slow, cautious, barefoot steps, the hush of skin on stone. No sound should carry such weight, but hers did. The weight of concern. Of someone small who shouldn't have had to learn it so young.

Her tiny hand pressed to my arm. Bare, bony. Needy, aching, starved for food, for comfort. As cold as the watching mountain. But still willing to give up what little warmth she had to someone else.

Why? Why was *she* the one comforting *me*? Why had this cruel world entrapped a spirit as bright and gentle as hers in a frame so fragile, ignored, and broken?

I had devoted myself to virtue, and yet I knelt, collapsed. She had known only abandonment, and yet she stood.

Where did that kindness come from? That wellspring of quiet love that defied her pain?

Maybe... maybe the kindest souls were not those who had never suffered, but those who suffered most. Maybe the ones who hurt the deepest were the ones most desperate to make sure no one else had to. Maybe that was what kindness truly was. Not an instinct, not a gift, but a rebellion.

And hers, the most beautiful I'd ever known.

A guttural "Ugh!" echoed through the chapel's doorframe. Sharp, disgusted, unmistakably Eryndra.

Her armor rattled with each heavy step, the scrape of her boots chasing her words down the aisle. "Right mess outside. Gerard looked like he was gonna piss himself," she muttered, her voice strained through exertion and irritation. "Demanded I leave post and come here at once. Said something about too... much...... light..."

She stopped.

I didn't need to see her. I could feel her silence. That moment where the room caved inward and nothing moved. I could feel her gaze land on the altar, the flickering teal. The realization that most of the blood on her feet didn't belong to the rioters. The ethereal body no longer golden, drenched and broken, laid like a votive offering before the silent god we still believed in.

A metallic clang shattered the stillness. Her shield hit the floor. Like the will to hold it had simply left her.

Her steps resumed, but slower now. Uneven. Her bones no longer knew how to carry her. That hesitance wormed its way into her voice.

"Daelon... is that...?"

I stared forward, my eyes still fixed on the body that had once been our center. Our song.

"It was," I said.

The body on the altar stirred, and the chapel held its breath. A low, ragged inhale, then she sat upright. Her gaze listed over the room in slow, tentative arcs, as though she were encountering the place for the first time. The fluid certainty of Kirtana was gone; in its place, her movements were hesitant: slowing, stiff, and burdened.

Her teal eyes passed callowly over us, as if we were part of the furniture. She glanced down at her arms, blood-darkened and heavy, the sight foreign to her. It was as if she'd awoken into someone else's body. Her posture slackened; shoulders hunched. Each movement required effort, as though gravity had doubled around her.

Then she stood.

The weight of every step echoed in the chapel's hush, each sluggish footfall a betrayal of her former floating grace. She lifted her gaze again to me, to Eryndra, as if trying to place us in her life anew. Her lips parted, hesitated. At last:

"I'm… not sure where I am," she said. Her voice was prickly to the ears, like a harp with broken strings. "Or... who I'm supposed to be."

She looked back to the altar, her expression blank, hollow. "This place... felt like sanctuary. I don't know that it is, anymore." Her words trembled with uncertainty, the conviction drained from each one.

Then she shook her head, as though to clear mist from her mind. She opened her mouth, and a barking scrape clawed erratically at the air, trying to find timbre. "I... I can't find the song." Her voice cracked. "I don't know how to sing anymore."

The awkward silence that followed was suffocating. A chasm between the sister we'd lost and the shadow left behind. A soul emptied.

Her teal gaze flickered toward Luna, who had edged forward, small hand extended in comfort. "Maybe I can teach you." Softly, the child began to hum a few hopeful bars; bright notes in the tension-choked air.

The moment a melody touched the stagnant air, the teal creature reacted. Her shape tightened, light spasming as though primed to snap. She lunged forward, swinging her arm back and forth in Luna's direction. "No! Stop it," she hissed, every word a warning.

Luna recoiled, pressing against my arm, crestfallen. Tears welled in her wide, innocent eyes.

Eryndra's armor scraped as she stepped between them. "Kirtana, that's enough," she said firmly. "The child meant no harm. Don't take your anger out on her."

The blue ethereal turned, her movements sluggish, resentful. A crooked finger pointed at Eryndra. "That's rich, coming from you, *soldier*," she spat, voice riddled with ice. "And don't ever call me by that name again."

Every word fell saturated with grief. The chapel's silence swallowed them. Kirtana's once-steadfast voice—uplifting, healing—had fractured completely. "The song is dead," she said. Her warped light shuddered. "*She* died with it."

Luna's little chest hitched as she broke into a sudden, wrenching sob. The sound filled the chapel like a wineglass cracked at its base. The blue ethereal narrowed her eyes, upper lip curling. Then she turned to me, and what light she had left seemed to withdraw behind those cold, distant eyes.

"Take that cursed thing and begone," she said, her voice dull but cutting. "It's clear you care more for it than your own family. Than your faith."

I flinched. Tried not to. Tried to remember the person she had been, and tell myself that this was grief speaking. That the teal shade of her light had corrupted her judgment, not revealed it. But her voice rang with a bitterness too precise, too tailored. She'd known just where to cut.

Eryndra met my eyes across the altar. It was clear that she was wounded, too. But she gave me the look. The one that meant she would handle it, but not with fists. With presence. With the full, unmoving mountain of herself.

That was enough.

I reached for Luna's hand—her cold, small, trembling hand—and led her quietly from the chapel.

10 - Tristessa Lethia

I guided Luna through the winding arteries of Rarek, unsure where I was going beyond the vague notion of "away." Away from the chapel. Away from that voice. From the blood. From the fractured memory of who my sister used to be.

The sun had long since abandoned the city, the thick curtain of night hanging overhead in its absence, but Luna didn't stumble. Her small hand remained in mine, damp from tears, but firm in her grasp. I looked down at her, and in the dim, her eyes glowed a vibrant pink, like paper lanterns floating on a still pond.

"You can see?" I asked gently.

She sniffled, rubbed her forearm beneath her nose, and gave a faint nod. "Mhmm."

She looked tired. Her steps were growing heavy, and every few paces she would lean just slightly more weight into my arm. It was late. Much too late for a child to be wandering the streets, glowing eyes or no.

I looked around to get my bearings, and spotted the ghaf tree. Still adorned with rich, thriving leaves despite the creeping cold of the season. It looked more out of place now than it had then. Vibrant in the frost, thriving when all else withered. A lie made of bark and bloom. A parasite from a foreign land.

And they let it root.

They let *him* root.

Vale stood beneath that tree and called it beautiful. He wasn't asking to belong. He was declaring that he already did.

And me? Raised in the marrow of this city's devotion. The chapel had stood long before the roots of that damned tree ever touched Rarek's soil.

But now I was the outsider.

They let him in. And they pushed me out.

It made me sick.

Still, the ghastly sight of it looming nearby meant we were close to the library. I wondered if Stetson might still be awake.

For the first time all day, the tide broke in my favor—we'd caught him just before he vanished into the night, the only fortunate thing to happen since I stepped back into Rarek. I called out to him and he started, scrabbling with his keys in one hand and the thick chair leg in the other. Moonlight licked dimly at his face as he squinted at us.

"Daelon?" he murmured, relief in his voice. "I'm sorry. I've closed up for the night."

I stepped forward, tone urgent but quiet. "I need a favor. The little one here," I nodded toward Luna, who shrank back and turned her glowing eyes downward, "she needs rest… and something to eat. Could we stay at your house tonight?"

Stetson's gaze flicked between me and Luna. Her shame, like a living thing, twisted in the air, and in my stomach.

He blinked in the dim light, warily studying us. "The inn's… full tonight?" he asked, brow furrowed.

I managed a soft, measured reply. "There's been an incident. We need someplace quiet, away from onlookers."

His eyes, now flicking over my arms and legs, hesitated. Blood-spattered and soaked. I must have looked a wreck.

Stetson swallowed, the weight of the situation pressing against his bulbous features. After a long moment, he locked the library door behind him, key turning with a final click. His shoulders slumped, but he nodded. "All right. Come with me."

He led us through the dark streets at a careful pace, his steps deliberate. Without a lantern, he clutched the broken chair leg like a torchless sentinel, squinting into the shadows. "You can't brighten that glow of yours a little?" he asked over his shoulder.

"Trying not to draw attention," I muttered.

That was all it took. He nodded, judgment dissolving, and said no more.

We reached his home: a modest structure tucked behind a crooked alley, worn but well-kept. He unlocked the door, ushered us in, then turned the key again behind us. A lantern was lit, casting warm hues over the neat space, and he crouched before the hearth to coax a fire to life.

"Is there somewhere we can wash up?" I asked, glancing down at the dried blood on my arms.

He pointed across the room to a wooden basin beside a pump drawn from the well. "There."

I drew up the water and nodded to Luna. She approached without a word, the kind of tired that sank deeper than her skin. She washed the dirt from her arms, then her hands, then splashed her face, finishing with a few greedy gulps. Not the order most people would follow, but I doubted anyone had ever taught her. When she finished, she moved to the fire and curled beside it like a stray animal who wasn't sure it had permission to stay.

Stetson was at the counter, chopping carrots and rootstocks with a measured rhythm. I didn't ask what he was making. I didn't care. The motions were what mattered: quiet, methodical, grounding. I didn't plan on eating anyway.

I turned back to the basin. The wrappings on my arms were stiff with dried blood, rust-colored and cracked like old bark. I unwound them slowly, careful to keep my glow as dim as I could manage. I didn't want to blind anyone. I also didn't want to look at myself.

The linen hit the water with a heavy, reluctant splash. I started to scrub. Dunk. Wring. Repeat. The rhythm wasn't as smooth as Stetson's, but it was mine. The blood seeped out in cloudy ribbons. I didn't stop. I didn't let myself think.

Kirtana. Or what remained of her. The men, one of whom might still be lying on the chapel steps, slowly leaking into the dirt. Vale, who had orchestrated all of this with the smile of a man pretending to be a savior. I could see right through him, and he knew it, and it didn't matter. Because no one was going to take my word over his.

I scrubbed until my fingers ached, until the water turned the color of old wine, until the fabric went from maroon to something closer to pink. The copper stench faded, but the stain itself wouldn't leave. Not fully. It never would.

At least my verses had survived. Most were etched onto the cloth that covered my face and chest, too far for the blood to reach. I didn't like writing on my arms and fingers, as they got the most wear. Even with all the misfortune, the only passage that suffered was one I had written myself, lost beneath the burn marks from where I'd held Luna. I didn't remember the exact phrases. Something about caring even when it hurt. The irony nearly made me laugh. For now, it still felt salient enough to avoid an immediate recreation. I'd rewrite it eventually.

Stetson scraped the pile of chopped vegetables off his cutting board and into an iron pot. He carried it to the fire and set it down gently, stirring with a long-handled spoon as the first bubbles began to roll. The smell of earthy, savory herbs and rootstock rose along with the steam.

I moved to the basin again, turning my attention to the cloth around my feet and lower legs. The stone was cool beneath me as I pulled the wrappings free. The blood here was less caked, more smudged and spattered, and it came off easier. Still, I scrubbed it with the same conviction, as if thoroughness could substitute for penance.

For asking her to sing. For not being here when Rarek needed me. For chasing silence on mountaintops while my sisters shouldered collapse alone.

For failing to bring back even a whisper of the one who made us.

When I finished, I lifted the basin and stepped outside to empty it into the gutter. The night air had cooled further, crisp and biting, and for a moment I welcomed it. An uncomplicated sting, unlike the day's wounds. I dumped the water, watched the red traces snake away in the dirt, and then went back inside.

The warmth hit me first, followed by the smell. Stetson was already ladling soup into two wooden bowls, handing one down to Luna. She beamed, a light kindling behind her eyes, and clutched the bowl with both hands like it might disappear.

She didn't wait for it to cool. She blew across the surface once, then took a sip that scalded her tongue. Her whole face twisted, but she didn't stop. She just puffed harder, mumbling thanks around too-hot mouthfuls. "This is really good," she said, glancing up at Stetson with wide eyes. "Like… really, really good."

Stetson, face unreadable, handed her a chunk of crusty bread with a soft grunt, then lifted his own bowl and turned to me. He jerked his head toward the next room. I put the basin down, puzzled, and tilted my head. Why?

He tapped the side of his ear with one finger, then traced a line in the air beside it with exaggerated care. His eyes turned toward where Luna was sitting in front of the fire, her back to us.

I followed his gaze. Her pointed ears were twitching. Small, reactive movements, flicking subtly every time we shuffled, even at the ones we thought were silent. Street instincts coupled with Elven physiology.

He wanted to speak without her hearing. I followed him into the next room. He closed the door softly behind us, the click of the latch unnervingly loud in the hush that followed.

He exhaled like he'd been holding his breath the entire walk from the hearth. Then, he muttered, "Stories didn't lie. Lilac skin. Hair like spring grass." There was something almost reverent in his voice at first, but the wonder twisted quickly into something sterner. He straightened, turned to face me fully, and dropped the softness from his tone.

"You brought a powder keg into my house," he hissed.

I blinked. "What?"

He didn't wait for me to stumble through the confusion. "Covered head to toe in brands," he continued, whisper-shouting now. "The kind the guild uses on apostates. On unstable sorcerers. Criminal mages. People the council doesn't trust."

I still didn't understand. "Aren't they just to mark them as dangerous? To visibly exile them?"

"They're not *just* signs of guilt," he said, "They're cages. Magic manacles. And when they break... they don't just fall off. They explode." He glared at me like I'd brought a lit torch into a hayloft. "Why in the gods' names does she have *that many*? Two dozen, at least!"

"Stetson, you can't seriously be concerned that she's dangerous..."

"Someone was!" he shot back. "You don't carve two dozen kill-switches into a person unless you're more afraid of what's inside them than what happens when they all go off at once!"

I just stood there. The heat behind his words didn't make them easier to accept.

"Brands aren't warnings, Daelon," he added. "They're traps. Contingencies. Magic fail-safes. That's how the guild deals with dark summoners. You don't banish what they bring up. You make sure they die before they let it through. The moment she draws on whatever they sealed off, those brands are designed to kill her."

I thought of the alleyway. Of her sobbing, her marks glowing like forge fires, the heat they threw off. How I could barely hold her. Had she been close to breaking them, then? I kept the thoughts to myself. I didn't want to stoke Stetson's worry.

He sighed and pinched the bridge of his nose. "Look. I already said she could stay the night. I'm not going back on my word. But you two are gone come morning. Don't bring her back here, and don't take her near the library. I've got enough trouble from firebrand yokels without some ward of the state threatening to blow the roof off the place."

I said nothing. Just nodded and moved for the door.

His hand landed on it before I could turn the knob. "If she goes, she'll take half of Rarek with her. Maybe more."

I wanted to call him paranoid. Dramatic. But I didn't. Because I didn't know. I'd never seen a branded sorcerer come apart at the seams.

But what possible threat could one small child pose to an entire enclave of ancient elves or an entire guild's worth of trained sorcerers? What could have scared them enough to etch her execution into her skin, and so many times over?

I walked back into the main room. She was curled up like a cat, knees drawn close, arms folded in tight. The fire's glow wrapped around her like a second skin. Beside her, the empty bowl she'd made quick work of still steamed faintly from the broth trapped within the wood. Her face twitched often, the line between peace and fear blurred beneath her brow. One moment serene, the smile of a person who'd eaten their fill, the next twisted into a tight grimace of someone pursued, then back again. Nightmares and sweet dreams rolled into one.

I didn't wake her.

There was a bed meant for guests in the other room, and I wouldn't be using it. But the fire had claimed her. Let it keep her safe for a little while longer. If she stirred, I would help her find the mattress.

I sat nearby, not too close, and unwrapped a thin strip of cloth from around my neck. I withdrew a pen from my pack, the ink as black and cold as the sky, and began to write.

In the quiet morning hush, Stetson handed me a slip of parchment. A few markings, the shape of a range, a note about where the sun would be at the river's bend. The enclave's supposed location, though he never said the word. He didn't have to. His eyes did the speaking: narrowed with caution, lined with the wish that we would leave soon. His movements were brisk, efficient. He rushed us to the door with talk of needing to open the library, though I knew it was closed today. I let it go. Luna, seemed immune to the unspoken tension. She leaned into gratitude, giving thanks in triplets while bobbing up and down.

Stetson smiled, or tried to, his lips pulling flat more than up, trying to force politeness over the weight of his unease. His eyes lingered on Luna, then drifted to me. Fear, maybe. Or guilt. Perhaps both.

Then he turned back toward his house without watching us go.

I nudged Luna along gently, telling her we should go check on my sisters at the chapel. Her expression dipped for just a moment, concern flickering like a candle in a draft. But it passed. She nodded, and followed.

The chapel looked cleaner than it had any right to. Someone had tried to erase the memory of what happened. The body was gone. Most of the blood washed away. Eryndra hated cleaning anything that wasn't her shield. She must have also needed something to scrub last night to occupy her mind. Only the cracked stone in the doorframe, where I'd driven a man's skull into it, remained untouched. Too deep to polish out.

The place felt quieter than usual, as though it too was still processing the weight of the day before.

Inside, only Eryndra stood watch, posted like a stone sentry before the shrine. Her shoulders squared, arm instantly shifting to raise her shield as we entered. Once she recognized it was us, her posture didn't soften so much as realign back to simmering vigilance.

"Where is everyone?" I asked.

She huffed. "Everyone," she repeated, stretching the syllables like they were foolish on their own. "Only ones who ever come here to pray are Selma and her husband. He's taken ill recently, so she's been staying at home nursing him."

I closed my eyes and exhaled. That wasn't what I'd meant. But she'd answered the question I asked, so I couldn't fault her for that. The words came again, firmer this time. "Where is *Kirtana*?"

"*She*," Eryndra bit, "doesn't go by that anymore. She's at her house. Wallowing in her own self-pity. She won't even tell me what happened. But it doesn't seem like she's a danger to herself or anyone else, so there's no point in me babysitting. I certainly wasn't about to leave the shrine unattended all night just to hear her whining and moaning with that scratchy new voice of hers."

"Sympathetic as always," I said, the sarcasm slipping out before I could stop it.

"Not like you stepped in to help." My spine stiffened. Again, my fault. I couldn't blame her for meeting ire with ire.

"Do you think *she* beat those men to death?"

That stopped her. The implication clicked. Her jaw slackened, just briefly, before her gaze dipped to my hands. I lifted them, still deeply stained.

"This is her blood," I said. "I tried."

Eryndra's eyes faltered, her voice softening just enough to be real. "I didn't know..."

But the softness cracked. Her mask reset. "Maybe it would've been better if she'd died."

The life seemed to leave Luna's body, and she curled her arms close to her chest.

I shook my head. "You don't mean that."

Normally, I would have agreed. Hollowing was a fate worse than death. But I hadn't accepted that she was gone. Not yet.

Eryndra saw it. Read the hesitation in my face. "You deal with her, then," she shot back. "Go see for yourself."

"Hey," I said quietly nudging Luna's shoulder. "I'm going to check on my other sister. Make sure she's alright."

Her eyes lifted to mine, wide, a little anxious. I softened. "She's been… feeling strange lately. Might not be herself. So I think it's better if you stay here for a little while."

"Okay," she said. "Will you be back soon?"

"Of course."

I turned to Eryndra, whose expression had already soured at the implication.

"You're not doing anything right now," I said. "Can you keep an eye on her?"

"What? No. I don't... what am I supposed to do with it?" she snapped, gesturing vaguely at Luna like she was a fish flopping in the grass.

"Just… answer her questions. Try to have some fun."

She looked at me like I'd asked her to swallow nails. "I don't do fun."

"Well, do your best impression."

Her lips curled, a vein attempt to project the grimace as a smile.

"I won't be long," I said.

I turned before she could argue again. Behind me, Luna chirped at her, "Do you really wear that much armor all the time? Doesn't it itch?"

Eryndra talked through her teeth. "Not as much as children do."

I knocked, gently at first, then louder. No answer.

I tested the handle: unlocked.

The door creaked open. The house smelled clean enough. But it felt wrong. Not like a graveyard, where splashes of colored flowers, visitors, and memories kept a sliver of hope and happiness tied to the quiet earth. This was colder. Sterile. A morgue. No fond memories here, no legacy, just absence. The absence of someone who used to matter. Who used to be.

She was in the corner, sitting in a chair. She was deathly still, as if she'd never moved from that spot. Her hand cradled her head, elbow on the armrest, hiding her eyes. She didn't look up. Didn't speak.

The blue light bleeding from beneath her wrappings was steady but cold. Like frost coating the edges of the room.

Kirtana always moved with rhythm—never idle, never stiff. Even when she sat, there was grace in it. Quiet purpose in the line of her back, cadence in the way she'd turn to speak. It was never a song, not literally, but it felt like one. Like the room shifted in her presence.

Now, the air was static. Still. As if nothing dared make a sound.

I stayed near the doorway. Didn't dare cross the threshold into whatever realm she now occupied. I wasn't sure she'd even heard me. Or maybe she had, and just didn't care.

My voice cracked the silence, uncertain and soft. "Kirtana?"

It was like I'd set a chisel to stone. She didn't flinch, didn't jolt. Just… folded in on herself, slow and deliberate, as if the sound had pierced something central. Her voice emerged from the folds of her hand, rough and slow like bark peeling from a tree.

"Don't call me that," she said. "She is the song. I am not her."

"Eryndra told me as much," I replied. "What should I call you then, sister?"

She sat quiet for a moment longer. Then, as if the words themselves were heavy in her mouth, she said: "Tristessa Lethia."

I chewed on it, slow. "Tristessa… sadness. Lethia… forgetfulness." I paused, hearing it in full for the first time. "Or melancholy oblivion."

She raised her head just enough for the light beneath her wrappings to catch on her trembling jawline. "Look at all Kirtana's faith has wrought. All her devotion. Look at what it built."

I stepped in, gently. "It built sanctuary. Community. A place where people could come and remember what it meant to believe in something. You gave them that. Every hymn, every line you stitched into the tapestries—"

She cut me off. "And for what? The chapel's empty. The people are gone."

"You kept it alive. You kept them coming back."

She still refused to look at me. "Did I? Did I *keep them*? Then where are they now?"

She waved her other hand, as if brushing away smoke. "Let the last three Tormites and the propagandized mob have their way with that place. I'll not lift another finger for them."

"There are still four of us in Rarek. Me. Eryndra. Selma. And her husband."

She barked a bitter laugh. "You barely count as a resident. And he has the fever. He won't live the week."

I tried to find some thread to hold. "There are still pockets out in the world. Hamlets where the old rites endure."

"And what good are they?" she snapped. "Scattered and weak while the heart of the faith dies choking."

She leaned harder into her hand. "You remember how many Ethereals once walked these streets. The two dozen of us that once kept vigil in Rarek? They fled. All of them. Ran while they still could. Cowards."

A pause. The venom in her voice left as tears dripped through her fingers. "Maybe they were right."

Her fingers curled against her head. "Maybe running was the smart move. What did our devotion buy us? Pain. Isolation. The privilege to witness the death of our faith first hand."

I couldn't speak.

"And what of you, brother?" Tristessa whispered. "Will you stand against the tides of change as apathy continues to morph into hatred? Will you intervene again, if the non-believers return with more blades, or fire? Will you become a hypocrite, reciprocating hatred while calling it righteousness, like our sister? Will you cling to your outdated ideals to maintain some illusion of purity that the unenlightened will ignore?"

The silence after her voice died was vast. It took everything in me not to reach for the easier answers. Not to justify, to argue, to meet grief with grief.

She finally looked up, fixing her hopeless blue eyes upon me. "How much does that golden light mean to you? How much will you sacrifice?"

I said only the one thing I still knew to be true.

"Everything."

She scoffed. A dry sound like crumpling parchment. It didn't belong in her throat, not in the body that used to carry notes like candlelight across the chapel's vaulted dome. But then, it wasn't Kirtana scoffing. Maybe that was the point.

"Some things never change," she said, eyes settling on the far wall. "Must be nice."

"It isn't," I replied. "I simply don't have a choice."

Her head turned. Slowly. The weight of it dragged her whole body into the motion, as if even that small act of engagement cost more than it should. The way she looked at me... so unbearably sad... felt like being lowered into icy water. It left a numbness behind. Her voice came quiet, nearly cracking, eroded.

"You *pretend* that you don't have a choice." Her gaze drifted downward, to her blood-caked hands. "You always choose this… *mission* of yours over us."

"I choose faith," I said, steadying myself against the gravity. "And while I respect that you and Eryndra have different opinions on what that means, I will not apologize for mine."

"Faith..." she echoed, as if the word had once been precious, and now tasted of ash. "Faith brings people together, Daelon. It makes life easier. It helps endure hardship."

She paused, letting her judgment sink in.

"Your faith has done nothing but isolate you. Make things harder. Hurt you. Hurt us."

"You're right," I said, soft but unmoved. "It does isolate me, by separating and defining me. It helps me endure. There is beauty. Maybe not in voices lifted, but those preserved in the script. In deciphering its meaning. In remembering the truth, even if I'm the only one left who believes in it."

Her face dropped. As if I had just told a mother her child wouldn't be coming home. Not today. Not ever.

She raised her hands to her elbows and began to unwind them. The bloodstained strips pulled away like old bandages, slow and deliberate, revealing the eerie cyan glow beneath. Kirtana always kept her verses from our creator on her arms. It was only there, written where she could see it, read it, trace it like a prayer. She'd never wanted to hide her face behind it.

The wrappings slipped from her fingers when she reached the last, tumbling through the stagnant air toward me. A lazy gust from the open door caught them and carried them halfway across the room before they landed. A discarded skin, molted as though it would never be needed again.

"You can lay it down too, brother," she said. Her voice was almost inviting. "It's just that easy. No one will fault you."

That tore something open in me. A silence roared between us.

I stepped into the house. Two paces. No more. I knelt and picked up the cloth, still damp at the seams, still smelling faintly of rust and fear. I didn't speak. Just wound them, slow and careful, around my own arms. The script beneath would need cleaning, maybe restoration, but that wasn't the point.

"I can't," I finally said. My voice sounded older than it had a moment ago. "And if I have to carry yours too… so be it."

She didn't look up. I turned and left.

11 - Behind the Mask

The instant I stepped back into the chapel, I could see Eryndra was near her wit's end. She didn't slouch—she'd rather die than show weakness—but her jaw clenched, her eyes were tight, and she held her shield like a fence, creating a physical boundary. Luna sat on the floor with her knees drawn up, chin on them, not crying or pouting, just small and quiet. The kind of quiet that came after trying and failing to make a friend.

The tension in Eryndra's frame softened when she saw me. Not into warmth, but something like relief. Her eyes said it all: *please take her.*

I looked to Luna. The tattoos that curled down her arms, legs, and neck were flickering again. Quick arcs of arcane energy darted laps around the perimeter of one sigil or another and then vanished. Like an ant skimming a ring of water. Blazingly fast, probably easy enough for most to dismiss as a trick of the light. She was quite greasy, after all.

I crouched beside her. "Hey. How do you feel about taking a little trip?"

Her head lifted slowly. There was hope in her face, but not the kind that jumped up and down. "Where to?"

"It's a surprise," I said. "It'll take a couple weeks to get there, but if we leave today, we could be back before Remembrance." I had no intention of bringing her back to this forsaken city if I could help it, but I needed an out in case we never found the veil.

"Is it far?" she asked.

"Have you ever walked a long way?"

She perked up. "Me and my sister ran the whole length of the Wayward Falls and back once."

"Is that far?"

She nodded like it was nothing. "'It's about thirty miles, depending on what time you leave."

I blinked. Strange fae things within the enclave, I supposed. We would have to travel much farther than 30 miles, but if she could run that far, walking shouldn't be too much of a problem.

Her gaze drifted a little, touched by memory. Whatever the Wayward Falls were, the thought of them hadn't hurt. That was good. I didn't say more. I just reached out a hand. She took it.

I gave Eryndra a nod. She returned it, gruff and short, but it said more than words ever could. My face, I knew, carried the weight of having gone to see Tristessa. She saw Kirtana's wrappings around my arms, and her eyes told me she understood. There was no blame in that moment, just the steady exchange of two siblings bound by duty, even when it hurt. My silence offered a non-apology. I was leaving again. Her fingers curled tighter around her shield. She didn't intend to back down from her post.

I took Luna by the hand and led her back into the city's churn. If we were going to make this trip, we'd need supplies. For her, mostly. I could travel with next to nothing: no food, no water, no bedroll, no cloak. Even torches were more a convenience than necessity for me. Luna, on the other hand, was all need and no preparation.

We'd have to rest often, too. For the most part, there'd be no horses, no carts heading our way. No trade road to ride. Just the two of us, walking into the wilderness.

Yet with Luna beside me, and fires sure to be lit for her warmth, I doubted we'd be bothered. Two figures casting shadows, a crackle in the dark—plenty to dissuade prowlers. Even when I traveled alone, my glow was usually enough to keep all but the boldest wildlife at bay. The curious ones never lingered long, too skittish to get close, especially if I made a sudden movement.

The city, for once, seemed calm. No shouting, no crowds, no sermons from atop some makeshift pulpit. No overconfident teens spitting in the face of someone twice their size. But the silence wasn't peace, it was posture. The looks told me as much. Lips curled, noses scrunched, shoulders turned as I passed. They didn't scream. They didn't strike. But they'd all sipped poison from Vale's cup. And now they measured me from afar, like something sticky they'd rather not step in.

I supposed that as long as they could ignore me, they didn't feel the need to silence me like they had Kirtana.

Their quiet prejudice seemed to dissolve the moment coin entered the conversation. Righteous scorn, it turned out, had a price. Aurelian had them convinced they were destitute, yet still found the means to get them to fill his coffers. It was a remarkable grift, really. Deprive them, then sell them deliverance with the coin they didn't have.

The shopkeeper at the general store was unshaven, and wore the weary bitterness of a man who'd been made to feel owed. He grumbled sideways as he tallied up my requests. Something about paying him with his own coin. Vale's lie again: that the church drained Rarek's taxes to fund its tiny shrine. As if any of us had seen a clipped copper from the city's treasury. What would we even do with it? Replace the windows?

Still, that coin was going somewhere. If not to the treasury, to Vale's personal stash. Its absence could be felt in the shopkeeper's gruff body language.

He squinted at the list. Rations, tinder, waterskins, salve, a warm blanket.

"Didn't think you cloth-skinned lamps needed any comforts," he muttered, eyeing me without shame.

I didn't rise to it. Just motioned down to Luna.

"They're for her."

He leaned forward over the counter, craning to see her, then gave a derisive snort. "Course the city can afford charity for the elves."

How anyone in Rarek could cling to bigotry was beyond me. A city as varied as a patchwork quilt, stitched with several dozen cultures, creeds, and lineages. Tribalism here would necessitate being angry or frightened nearly every waking hour. And still, this man found reason to voice his discontent aloud, while depending on their business. If he'd been younger, or stronger, maybe he'd have said more. The capital sometimes maintained its civility through self-policing. People who said truly provocative things had best be prepared to defend their hatred, or learn how to take a punch.

But shame and violence could only deter so much. Otherwise, Eryndra would have beaten the entirety of Rarek into submission.

Grumbling as though I'd twisted his arm, the shopkeeper gathered the items I'd asked for and slid them across the counter, one by one, as if each was an offering extracted by force. He bit every coin before letting it vanish into the till, grimacing when they all passed muster. At last, with a nod sharp as a dismissal, he "allowed" us to leave his shop.

Luna lingered for a second, a furrow in her brow as she glanced from him to me. But I gave no reaction; just shouldered the pack. She mirrored my calmness, small and observant, and we walked on.

My satchel felt fuller than it ever had, packed tight with the things she'd need. Rations, warmth, water, tinder. Nothing heavy enough to slow me, but enough to remind me I wasn't walking alone anymore.

The day ahead was bright and sunny, a welcome contrast to the hazy bitterness festering under the red and gold banners. We stepped through the front gate. This time, its wide open span made it seem as if the city hoped to be rid of things more than it hoped to welcome them.

After taking enough steps that it would be inconvenient, or at least telegraphed, if I took offense: a few voices called out after us from somewhere safely tucked inside the walls.

"Good riddance!"
"Don't come back!"
"And stay out!"

Empty threats made by people far enough away to be safe. Unlike the city itself, which could be strong and resistant if ever it need be, the people within were weak, but wanted to project that same strength to hide their inadequacies.

Let them have their theater.

The first stretch of the road passed like a fable. Luna, boundless and bright, danced through the tall grass with a kind of reckless joy that made the landscape feel almost holy. She skipped ahead, chased butterflies, sang little tuneless songs to herself, and named rocks like they were old friends. The prairie welcomed her; she looked just as at home under the yawning sky as she had in the throngs of Remembrance. There was something in her bones that knew how to live, even if everything else about her was starved and quiet.

We stopped to eat when she grew hungry. She always offered to share, sometimes pouting if I didn't partake. I'd pretend to nibble, breaking off the smallest pieces I could, chewing long to make them last. Considering we might need to walk back if the veil refused us, I couldn't risk waste, no matter how much her enthusiasm tried to feed me.

She only asked where we were going a few times. I never gave her the full truth, for fear of disappointing her if the veil wasn't there. Just said it was beautiful. She seemed content with that.

Though the season still clung to cold, and she shivered easily when moving slowly, she often refused the blanket. It puzzled me. I always offered when I saw her tremble, but she only took it occasionally, seemingly at random. There were no patterns, no rules. Just a strange resistance to comfort. I'd never known a child to deny warmth.

At night, we stopped. I made fires. She curled up beside them. Twice, when the wind was mild, I carried her through the night. She never stirred, even as I walked for hours. She weighed scarcely more than my pack. I tried not to steal any of her warmth, even when I wanted to. She needed it far more than I did.

The moment we stopped, just as the sun dipped behind the hills and bled the last light into the sky, I knew something felt off. We were close now. We'd veered from the trade roads a couple days back. No more cobbles, no markers, no signs of life but our own footprints in the soil. Just plains and occasional forest, open sky above. Untamed wilderness.

Luna sat beside the fire, humming a little tune as the food cooked, when her ears gave a sudden twitch. Then another. Her whole posture went stiff, alert, and her eyes widened as she turned toward the trees. I followed her gaze and listened. Crackling fire, wind in the grass, but beneath it... rustling.

Just beyond the firelight, I saw them. Eyes. Scattered along the woodline like tiny, hungry lanterns. My heart sank. Wolves.

Damn it!

Even the curious ones usually turned from a glance. Now we had fire, two bodies, and still they came. Why?

As the smell wafted under my nose again, it hit me. The food. When I traveled alone, I never cooked. Never needed to. The smell must've carried for miles.

Three wolves stepped from the trees, ribs jutting against their pelts. Hungry. Desperate. They fanned out slowly, heads low, watching our every movement.

"Back!" I barked at them, yanking a wrap from my hand and letting the light flare out. They flinched, blinking, but didn't retreat. I grabbed a burning stick from the fire and hurled it. One shifted aside but didn't run. They were too lean to leave a potential meal behind.

"Luna, get behind me. Cover your eyes."

She darted over and dropped to her knees behind me, tucking herself tight against the backs of mine. I felt her arms rise, shielding her face the way I'd told her.

"No peeking," I said. "No matter what."

I pulled the wrappings loose. First my face, then neck, shoulders, and chest, unveiling the light until it spilled out in blinding waves. The wolves emerged in full view, ragged and wild, each strand of their matted fur clinging to them like brittle weeds. Still, they pressed forward, blinking against the glare, heads lowered but noses twitching with hunger.

I turned, keeping Luna between me and the fire. Even starved, these beasts were almost twice her size. If they made a break for her, I'd have seconds. Maybe less.

I turned the light up, high enough that it clawed at my own eyes, but they kept coming. One growled. The sound wasn't loud, but it carried a signal to the others.

They came all at once, snarling and snapping with the frenzied abandon of beasts who'd already decided they were dead if they failed.

The first leapt for my throat, and I caught it midair by the neck. The second clamped onto my outstretched arm, its weight wrenching me downwards. The third came low, head ducked, jaws gaping for whatever soft target it could find below my waist. I turned my hip and drove my heel into its snout, knocking it sideways with a yelp and a spray of spit. It skulked back into the dark, growling in frustration.

The one on my arm shook violently, trying to tear loose the muscle beneath. But I had no time to scream. My grip tightened on the first wolf's neck as it flailed, and with my free hand I reached for the second's skull, fingers finding the narrow ridge of bone between its eyes.

Its pupils were pinpricks. Madness stared blindly back at me.

I pressed down on the bridge of its nose, blocking the airway. Desperation clawed at its limbs as its instincts shifted. Hunger could overrule fear, but not suffocation. Its jaw slackened. I yanked its head free and flung it round into the fire. It struck and overturned the pot, skidding across the coals.

The yelp it gave was so shrill I felt Luna wince. It scrambled, scorched legs kicking wildly as it fled the firepit, vanishing into the dark.

I turned, still gripping the first by the neck. Its thrashing had slowed, but it hadn't surrendered. It continued snapping at my face, and I drove a fist into its temple. I leaned forward, slamming it to the ground with the weight of my whole frame. My fist met its skull again and again, each impact duller than the last as its flailing turned to twitching, then to a spasming crawl toward unconsciousness.

Then a scream. High, sharp, close.

My head snaped back. The third one, the clever one, had come back around. With the embers scattered and our attention fractured, it found its window. It had Luna by the arm, hauling her backwards into the dark. Her face was screwed tight, eyes shut as I'd told her. I was amazed she was still following that order.

I surged to rise, but my leg jerked back like it had snagged a root. I glanced down.

The first wolf, the one I'd just beaten near death, had latched onto my ankle with its final shred of will. Blood streamed from its temple, one eye shut and concaving. And still it clung.

Luna screamed again, the sound thinning with distance.

Whatever decency remained in me vanished. I raised my other foot and brought it down, heel first. Bone crunched, surrendering its shape. The bite released.

I left it behind without a glance. My body blurred with motion, chasing the drag-marks, the rustling, the thin wail of a child being stolen into shadow.

I broke through the treeline, my searing light revealing the grappling pair. Twelve steps away. The burned wolf, three paces from the melee, had also made a comeback. It was going to reach them before I could. I ran as fast as my legs would carry me, but it had too much of a head start.

Ten steps away.

It bit her other arm, and the two wolves started to pull in opposite directions. She screamed, my ears bleeding along with my heart.

Eight steps away.

Luna's tattoos stirred to life, rippling like centipedes and turning an eerie red. Blood rolled down each of her arms as they jerked and pulled on her.

Six steps away.

The markings flared, not just alive but raging. Infernos coiling across her skin. I could hear the wolves' mouths sizzling, the sickening sound of their insides cooking. They didn't let go.

Four steps away, and my arms stretched, uselessly, trying to leap the rest of the distance for me.

She screamed, and threw open her eyes. A magenta-colored cone burst forth, swallowing the first wolf in an instant. Its yelp cut off as its body turned to cold, lifeless stone. Her head turned, dragging the arcane beam with it, and the second wolf met the same fate. A whimper, a jerk, and it froze mid-pull, calcified into an eerie statue with an unsettling level of detail.

But her head kept turning.

The pink ray followed the motion, sweeping toward me.

I didn't have time to react. I slammed my eyes shut, bracing for the moment my body would succumb. Then another scream tore from her lungs, the sound somehow different.

I opened my eyes.

Her head was thrashing violently, the arcane light gone. Her eyes blinked rapidly, washed out and searching, focusing on nothing. My light was still burning brightly. Remorse punched through me as I turned it down, covering myself as quickly as my fingers allowed. I rushed toward her, sick with fear.

She had looked straight at the light. At *me*.

She thrashed, caught between the jaws of the two lifelike statues, their stone teeth still deep in the tissue of her tiny arms. Her cries cut through the night louder than the wolves ever had. I ran to her, dropping to my knees.

"It's okay, Luna. It's okay. You're safe now. You're safe." I whispered it again and again, but she wasn't listening. Her panic had deafened her. I reached to touch her shoulder, but the brands screamed my mistake back at me. White-hot agony seared into my palm and I pulled back.

"Luna, please. It's me. It's Daelon. You're safe. You're okay. You're okay!" I pleaded.

Nothing. The twisting red marks throbbed, gathering up the last slack from her skin to bulge ominously upward. Molten pustules on the verge of bursting.

She was hysterical. I needed to calm her down. I wracked my brain for what I could do short of trying to break the stone statues with my bare hands.

Why wasn't she phasing? She could fall through my arms, slip through solid rock—but she didn't. Her fear had locked her in place. And worse, the sizzle of burning flesh twisted my stomach. It wasn't just fear for what might happen if she continued.

It was what was already happening to her.

My gaze dropped, and there they were. My hands. Bandaged in the dried blood of a sister who had once been the voice of our people. Of beauty. Of peace. I clenched my fists around the linen, as if I could wring a miracle from them.

And then, softly—badly—I sang.

It was out of tune. Staggering. I tripped over the meter and forgot the next line more than once. Kirtana's wrappings had not passed down her gift. But they had passed down her will. Her heart. Her stubborn insistence that the light mattered, even if only in the attempt.

I remembered the verse, obscured beneath the blood, half-lost but still true.

"Make a joyful noise unto the stars, that they might remember we were here."

I sang it again. Again. Until the sound, as weak and graceless as it was, began to take root in the air. Luna's cries softened. Her body stilled. The tight lines of her face eased, the panic retreating like a tide. Her eyes, though blind and dazed, no longer darted.

She remembered Kirtana, too.

And slowly, mercifully, she came back to me.

The glow of her washed-out eyes returned slowly, as if they had to relearn their color. That brilliant pink bled back into the whites in a cautious seep, as if afraid of what it might see. Her pupils were still pinpricks, hiding the scene from her. I hoped her vision would return. I couldn't bear the thought of having blinded her, even partially.

Blood still fell from the jagged wounds left behind by the wolves' stone jaws, but it dripped slowly, instead of freely flowing.

The rage in her markings dulled, the heat waning until I dared place my hand on her shoulder again. She flinched, stiffened. The same frightened recoil from the carriage, back when I'd first earned her fear. But this time she remembered. Remembered what she could do.

With a faint breath, she loosened herself, letting her body phase just enough to slip through the frozen mouths. She fell limp against me, spent. I caught her, cradling her with more gentleness than strength. She needed peace. I still needed to fall apart. But I couldn't yet.

I carried her back through the trampled brush. Those twelve mile-long paces. I laid her down on the blanket next to the scattered embers. Her eyes fluttered. No sleep yet, just shock. I gathered the scattered logs, restacked them, and breathed life back into the fire. Even if the air didn't demand it, she always seemed to enjoy the warmth.

I reached into my pack for the salve, fingers moving with the mindless precision of ritual. I smeared the ointment thinly across strips of clean linen. I raised her tiny arms one at a time, wrapping the punctures with deliberate care. The wounds were brutal, but she didn't cry. It was a welcome respite from her screams.

A blessed hush.

Realizing what the attack had interrupted, I asked if she was hungry. That I would make her something to eat. She didn't answer right away. Just sat there, her eyes not quite landing on me. After a moment, she gave the faintest shake of her head.

'By Torm's mercy,' I thought, *'Let her sight return by morning. Let this not be the price of a single meal.'*

She curled into herself, moving with great care as she eased her bandaged arms into a fold that wouldn't put weight on the wounds. A small, deliberate shuffle. And then stillness.

She slept.

Thank the right hand of Tyr, she slept.

12 - Revelation

Luna woke with the kind of quiet energy that only children seem to muster after horror. Fragile, yet already looking for something new to anchor to. Her eyes had their color again. Bright, pink, and flecked with light like river stones. Normal, for her.

She sat up and inspected her arms, running tiny fingers along the bandages. Then she held them out, proud. "Now I'm like you," she said, smiling.

I smiled back, but no words followed. I didn't want to stain something so pure with the truth of it.

She glanced over toward the trees, where I'd spent part of the night burying the last wolf. Her finger rose, pointing to the edge of the wood. "Can we go see them?" she asked.

I should've said no. But I couldn't. I just nodded.

We walked into the trees, the daylight thinning beneath the canopy. The statues waited where I'd last seen them. Silent, contorted echoes of desperation. Their features still locked in twisted snarls, teeth bared, eyes wild with hunger. I could still see the blood on their jaws. Her blood.

Luna wandered close, inspecting them without touching. Her steps were slow, deliberate. Her head tilted this way and that, as though trying to understand not just what they were, but why.

Then she started crying.

I thought it was fear. A delayed wave of last night's terror finally catching up to her. But when she turned to face me, her cheeks already streaked with tears, she said something else.

"I'm sorry," she blubbered, barely getting the words through her shaking lips.

"What ever for?" I asked, bewildered.

She sniffled hard. "You told me not to look. No matter what. But I did. And now... now the doggies got hurt. I didn't mean to. Honest."

I blinked. For a moment I didn't know what to say. They had tried to kill her. To tear her apart. But that wasn't how she saw it.

I cleared my throat and swallowed the confusion. "I'm not mad," I said gently. "And… at least they won't be hungry anymore."

I reached out my hand. She stared at it, sniffling, glanced back at the wolves, then placed her tiny fingers into mine.

The last day of our journey passed beneath a quiet, overcast sky. The weight hanging between us had grown too dense to speak through.

She walked with her head down, the bounce gone from her steps, trailing half a pace behind me. I didn't rush her. I couldn't bring myself to.

I kept seeing it: those wolves frozen in anguish, the way her eyes had flared. That beam of searing magenta.

That moment had left a splinter in my mind. A fracture between the image I held of her and the terrifying, unearthly force that had erupted from her.

Lamia were creatures of fable, of fantasy. Stories used to terrify children against wandering into caves, women against infidelity, and men against lust. Monsters of coiling scales and horrid, impossible-to-behold visages. So horrid they turned any onlooker to stone. But just like angels, they were fiction.

Weren't they?

Luna looked nothing like how they were described. No scales, no fangs, no claws, no serpentine form, not revolting to look upon. But those statues were undeniable in their concreteness. Power feared by the guild, or perhaps the elves.

I thought of Stetson's face when he saw her in the firelight. The fear. The warning. Someone, somewhere, had believed she was a threat worth sealing with two dozen chains.

Those chains hadn't held. But they also hadn't killed her.

All that forbidden power, and not one of those death-sigils had gone off. Either the warding system had failed, or worse—that terrible, penal system had judged what she did as… permissible.

What gods-forsaken depth of magic had she been marked for, if *that* wasn't the trigger? What else lived behind those big, shimmering eyes? Myth and nightmare rolled into one trembling child.

I knew she wouldn't have the answers. Whatever she'd unleashed that night, her investigation of the wolves showed she clearly didn't understand it any better than I did.

A few hours past noon, we came upon a winding river. The current bent unnaturally along the horizon, more memory than geography. This was the last landmark, the final direction that pointed us to the veil's supposed location.

Luna's ears twitched. Her mouth parted. And she lit up like a sunrise. Recognition bloomed across her face. And before I could ask, she was already shouting.

"I *know* where we are!" she beamed, pointing ahead with both bandaged arms. "That's the Wayward Falls!"

Her stories came rushing back to me.

Where the waterfalls go sideways.

The river, of course. She vibrated with anticipation, hopping in place, and then shouted, "I can't wait to race my sister!"

There it was again. That little shard of hope too happy to die.

But that hope twisted something in me. If this was her fate: exiled and branded, then what of her sister? Was she even here? Had she suffered the same? Would she still recognize Luna? Still love her?

I didn't know. But I did my best not to show it.

"Do you know the way from here?" I asked.

She nodded, already turning. "Come *on*! We're almost there!"

And just like that, she took off along the riverbank, fast and wild as if nothing in the world had ever hurt her.

I had to push myself just to keep her in sight. As I struggled to keep pace, my foot caught a mound hidden beneath the curtain of wild blooms. I stumbled forward, nearly going down, but caught myself. A puff of dry soil burst up and stuck in my throat.

A few steps later, something prickled. Then again. Then everywhere. The burn started low and spread like flame licking at oilskin. I looked down. My legs, swinging between the peonies, were crawling with dark specks—hundreds of them,. each one expressing their collective vendetta. Fire ants.

The flowers bite.

I leapt into the river. The ants wouldn't kill me, but their venom burned. They could swim, of course, but I wasn't trying to drown them. I just needed them off, needed to scrub away the scent of that frenzy they carried. I walked a ways through the water, each step loosening another clump of angry hitchhikers, until the last few lost their grip.

When I stepped back onto the bank, further downstream, I looked up the trail.

Luna was gone. Of course she was.

I raced along the river's edge, sticking to the narrow line between grass and water, avoiding the flowers like they bore the plague. The ground blurred beneath me, the steady roar of the river a tether keeping me from panic.

A few miles on, I spotted her, just a glimpse of green, slipping into the mouth of a cave carved into the side of the riverbend.

"Luna!" I called.

She didn't answer. The sun had begun its slow descent, not yet reddened, but lower than I'd like for chasing shadows into unknown caverns. I followed anyway.

The entrance narrowed behind me as I stepped into the cave, the rush of the outside world vanishing the moment I crossed the threshold. The air inside was cool and moist, laced with the scent of wet stone and something faintly floral. The walls rose high above, curving like the inside of a great earthen cathedral, every inch of them cloaked in a thick, springy moss the color of soft jade. The ground had no bite or edge, just a gentle give, like walking atop the fuzz of childhood blankets. There wasn't a single patch of bare stone underfoot or on the walls. Even my feet, despite the wrappings, could tell—

Everything's soft there.

As I moved deeper, light filtered in through thin, hidden fissures high above, casting slow-moving shafts that drew my eyes upward. And the ceiling—by the gods...

It was layered in sheets of pale blue crystal, flecked with white and silver, catching the light from above and bending it all across the chamber. Ten thousand fractured skies captured in the prism overhead, moving and shimmering with the slow grace of clouds. The light shifted when I moved, but even if I stood still, the twinkling reflections captured the sun's angle as it dipped lower outside.

It's where the real sky is.

I understood, in that moment, what she meant. It wasn't just the color. It wasn't just that the specularity of the crystals mimicked the stars. It was the way everything in here seemed... untouched. As if the world outside was a pale imitation. A lesson scrawled in dust, and this was the handwriting of something sacred. And it stood silently, its visual majesty saying all that needed to be said, without uttering a single sound. Unjudging.

"A blessed hush..." I whispered.

Luna must have heard me. She came scampering out from around a bend up ahead, her bare feet pattering confidently over the moss. "Come on!" she chirped, already halfway to vanishing again. "Hurry up!"

I moved to follow, careful with each step. The ground here felt wrong for sound. Too sacred for the slap of boots. So I tried to soften my tread, as if I could carry my weight more gently just by willing it. There was only one part left to her little riddle, I thought.

She stopped by a monolith jutting from the floor—huge, sudden, and wholly out of place. Unlike the other stones, this one hadn't been touched by the moss. It stood raw and sharp, its edges chiseled to impossible precision. But it didn't look built so much as exhumed.

Luna skipped toward it with the same ease as before, her fingers brushing along its side, tracing patterns I couldn't yet make sense of.

Symbols crawled across its face. I didn't need to be a scholar to tell they were the same tongue as those on her skin.

"What is it?" I asked.

"It's the door!" she said, beaming, as if she'd just unveiled a carnival trick and not the culmination of some ancient, hidden rite. She held up her small hand, fingers splayed in the shifting light. As her arm rose, the sunlight filtering through the real sky above was caught and blocked, casting a narrow shadow that fell clean across one of the etched symbols.

The stone responded.

With a sound like a lock being spoken to, the monolith gave a mechanical groan and began to turn. I saw a new symbol appear on her forehead, unscarred like the others burned into her arms, legs, and neck. It shone in vibrant green. The same hue blazed from the twin rune etched into the pillar's side.

The sun remembers your name.

When the monolith had rotated halfway round, it clicked once more. A portal silently brought itself into being beside it. Not like the quivering rips the guild conjured. This was a fact, arriving late to a quiet place. The blinding white oval of light hovered in the air, sheer and smooth.

I lifted my hand to shield my eyes. The habit was instinct, but the guilt that followed wasn't.

It was beautiful in a way I'd never seen, yet instantly recognized. Like hearing a harmony you'd never sung, but somehow knew the shape of. If Torm's voice spoke the world into being, then perhaps this was the echo still ringing in the furthest corners.

Was this, too, part of Torm's creation? A truth we'd forgotten? A verse left out of the hymns? Or was it something else entirely?

And I stood there, ashamed that I'd flinched.

She darted forward, tugging hard at my arm. "Come on!" she chirped, her grip full of joy. But something in me stalled. A quiet tug in the gut, a wrongness I couldn't place. My heels stayed in the ground, but she pulled again, insistent. My feet begrudgingly gave up their stubbornness and started moving.

"I can't wait to see mom and da—"

She stopped mid-sentence, colliding with a tall, lithe figure stepping from the other side of the rift.

He was regal in the sterile, unreal way of paintings. A long, white robe hung from his frame like untouched parchment. His skin, a shade of lilac unmarred by tattoos, seemed too pristine to have ever suffered. His hair, a curtain of pale silver, fell in calm, weighted strands. And his eyes, deep blue and cold like the bottom of an arctic basin, stared through us both.

The long, thin tail behind him flicked once, twice, like a cow swatting at flies.

Luna blinked up at him. Her head tilted slightly, like she was listening for a sound that never came. No recognition stirred in her expression. She didn't know him.

And yet... he knew her. He said nothing at first. Just studied Luna with that unreadable, clinical gaze. "Impressive," he murmured, as though noting the results of a stray experiment. "That you found your way back here. I shall correct my oversight."

He didn't use her name. Didn't bend, didn't smile. Only lifted one long, glowing fingertip and made a quick swiping motion across her brow.

The green symbol vanished in a sharp, silent puff.

"Hey!" Luna shouted, as though she'd been flicked. She stumbled back a step and glared up at him. "You're being rude! Let us in!"

He shifted his eyes to me for the first time, as if only just now acknowledging I was present. "The Faelar family relinquished this child. She is no longer recognized by the enclave."

"*Relinquished?*" I echoed. "What do you mean?"

He tilted his head faintly, as if gauging whether I was simpleminded. "Relinquished," he said. "To cease to hold or claim. To renounce, to forsake, to abandon or surrender."

I rolled my eyes. That wasn't what I meant, but it WAS what I asked. I bit back the frustration and tried again.

"*Why* did they give her up?"

Luna's voice cracked through the cave's hush, barely more than a squeak. "What?" Her shoulders twitched like they might draw up to shield her ears. She was teetering, caught somewhere between defiance and despair.

The man didn't so much as glance at her.

His hand drifted lazily toward her, palm up, a loose gesture of presentation. "She was born under an astral convergence," he said, the words clipped clean of any sympathy. "The sect believed her presence invited calamity. That she might be a vessel for things best left unnurtured."

His face gave no hint of guilt, or pity, or apology. Only stillness, like the matter had already long been settled.

I stared at him, stunned. "They *abandoned* their child? Because of when she was born?"

Luna turned sharply at that, eyes wide and wild. "No," she insisted. "My sister—my sister was born at the same time I was. We have the same birthday!"

The man remained statuesque. "The Faelar's eldest daughter arrived two minutes before the celestial apex. She exhibits no signs of affliction."

Luna's face contorted. The hurt turned into rage.

"You're a liar!" she shouted, yanking on my hand and storming toward him. "I'm gonna tell on you!"

But he moved like a curtain of smoke. His arms rose, spreading wide, thin fabric drifting like wings in a nonexistent breeze. "Good day," he said with that same surgical tone, stepping backward into the white void. The rift sealed shut behind him.

The obelisk rotated with a slow, indifferent grace, settling back into place with the finality of a book being closed. The green glow was gone. Just dull stone and silence.

Luna ripped her hand from mine and stomped over to it, the soft moss muffling her furious steps. She raised her arm high, shadowing the same mark as before.

No click. No stir. The light that answered was not green, but red.

She tried again, this time harder, with force, lowering her arm and thrusting it back up.

Nothing.

"No…" she whispered.

I stared, frozen and helpless, as she tried a third time—shaky, more desperate—her hand held above her head. Still red. Still silent.

She stumbled over to the stone and collapsed against it, knees hitting the mossy floor with a wet thud. She pressed her small palm flat against the mark, her entire body shaking. "No, please," she pleaded.

Red light shone up between her fingers.

"I'll be good, I promise! PLEASE!"

Her hand struck the symbol again, harder now. The sound of skin on stone echoed softly through the cavern, but the pillar remained unmoved. The light stayed red.

Her forehead met the stone with a gentle thud. Then again, harder. And again, until her voice finally cracked beneath the weight she'd been straining to carry all this time.

It started with hiccuped breaths that couldn't decide if they were sobs or gasps, sharp little gulps caught in the throat. Then the dam broke—her whole frame shaking, curling in on itself as if to shield what little pride she had left from the truth's final, cruel blow. Her fists stayed planted on the stone, trembling, useless.

The sound of her crying was too big for someone her size. Wails like she was grieving not just her parents, but the very idea of love. The illusion that there was a place for her, somewhere. Someone. Her voice scraped out, each plea more broken than the last. "Please," she whimpered again, not even loud enough for the stone to hear. "Please…"

The soft moss beneath my boots, the crystal canopy overhead—mere moments ago, they'd captivated me with their majesty. Now, they meant nothing. The wonder of this place had been shattered by the sound of her breaking.

She belonged here. That had been clear the moment the gate opened. But someone told her she didn't. And now she believed them.

I wanted to go to her. To reach out. But the weight of this place, and of what she was feeling, held me still. What if my presence only made it worse? What if she looked up and saw in me the same outsider she now saw in herself?

I took a cautious step forward.

Her head dropped fully now, cheek pressed against the obelisk like it might change its mind if she could just touch it hard enough, long enough, lovingly enough. Tears puddled on the moss. Her breath came in short spurts, like her own body was trying to reject what had happened.

Like it couldn't possibly be true.

The girl who had skipped across fields had folded into something unrecognizable. A pile of sobbing cloth and shame. Her back rose and fell with each new wave of grief. Like it might never stop.

I wanted to hold her. To promise her something. Anything.

But what was left to promise?

Her tattoos were completely dark and dormant. No arcane tantrum or burning magical safeguard. This pain was real. Quiet. Crushing. Emotional. It came not from the cursed ink etched into her skin, but from the jagged, invisible fracture in her heart.

And that meant one thing: I could hold her. If she would let me.

I reached down, slowly, giving her every chance to pull away. But she didn't move. Not even an inch. Her fingers stayed curled against the stone, knuckles pale with pleading, though her arm had gone limp. I scooped her up, gentle as I could manage. She didn't fight it, just sagged into my chest like a wet rag. Her cheek pressed against the soft wrappings over my shoulder.

And so I carried her. Away from the monolith, away from the place that had betrayed her hope. Out into the waning sun, her weight heavy with sorrow. Three times heavier than she'd been before. But I didn't falter.

She needed me to be strong. That much, at least, I could do.

13 - Where is Home

I carried Luna north, the river murmuring softly beside us, until the cave was gone from view, tucked somewhere behind the trees and the bend. I made sure we were well clear of the peonies, then stepped toward the bank and lowered myself down, my legs sliding over the edge into the cool current. The water wrapped around my ankles, coaxing some measure of calm from the restless throb still pulsing against my chest.

Her head rested beneath my chin, hair catching wisps of river breeze. One of her small hands had found its way to my shoulder, limp but clinging faintly. The other curled into the folds of the wrap across my back like she was afraid she might float away if she let go.

I hated this moment.

And I never wanted it to end.

There was something sacred about it. Something cruel. The shape of her grief was unbearable, but the fact that I could hold her through it—that it helped—made me feel… worthy. Just a sense that I was needed. Useful.

Kirtana had been the song. Eryndra was the shield, and I the messenger. And this trembling girl who'd once asked me what my message was, what it meant to be me, had torn that question open again.

I still didn't know answer. And that terrified me.

Because for a heartbeat, I imagined a different kind of purpose—one shaped not by prophecy or faith or scripture, but by choice. By care. What if I let this become my new path?

But the thought shattered before it could form fully.

I couldn't imagine a world where I wasn't striving toward something more, seeking answers, trying to fulfill a purpose I didn't fully understand. That drive wasn't just spiritual. It was instinct. Like a compass embedded in my soul, fixed on a destination I couldn't name but could never stop chasing.

I had taken up Kirtana's bindings. To abandon them now, to abandon *her* so soon, would be to say her sacrifice meant nothing. I couldn't do that. I didn't know how.

When the last blush of sun had fled the sky and left only the hush of twilight behind, I rose. Her breathing was slow and steady now, the rhythm of exhaustion finally overtaking the chaos of sorrow. I shifted her gently, settling her against my shoulder so as not to disturb her hard-won sleep. She'd cried herself out. And though I felt a deep, aching gratitude that she'd found some semblance of rest, it twisted my insides to know what had purchased it.

I followed the river upstream, each step deliberate. The same miles she had sped through only hours ago now passed beneath me in silence. Her weight was no burden. If I could carry her where her feet could no longer take her, then so be it. If my arms could hurt in place of hers, I welcomed the pain. But it was the other kind: what twisted through her chest and flooded behind her eyes... that I wished I could lift instead.

My light was dim, just enough to trace the way forward. But where was I supposed to take her?

Rarek? The people had turned cruel—twisted by Vale's poison and their own festering fear. And if they tried to cage her, they'd learn no walls could hold a child who could phase through stone.

And once they realized that?

They'd do worse.

In the gentle glow, I saw the tattoos burned into her skin. Dormant, but alive. Watching me. They slithered beneath the light from my eyes, writhing like the ink had been dropped in water. If she couldn't stay safe in Rarek, Rarek itself wouldn't be safe.

Still, I kept walking. Back towards the only home I knew.

Eryndra was still in there. Wounded, angry, isolated. She might not have explicitly asked for help, but I couldn't leave her to bear the city's weight alone. I had to try—one last time—to salvage what was left of our family.

The next two days passed in a silence more consuming than any I'd known. She never once asked to be put down. Awake, she clung to me, light as ash but with the gravity of mourning, of a child untethered from everything that had once anchored her. Asleep, she folded into herself like parchment left out in the rain. Her breath came soft against my shoulder, as if the effort of dreaming cost her more than she could afford. Luckily, the nights were not cold enough to need a fire.

I tried to feed her. First with soft words, then quiet insistence. She only shook her head, barely a motion. Her lips, already pale, grew drier with each refusal. It unnerved me. She was already so slight, any thinner and she'd start vanishing entirely. But what could I do? I couldn't force her like she was some stubborn pet. I wasn't her jailor.

I kept her wrapped in the blanket when the winds picked up, kept her close when she trembled. I knew the only reason I could hold her like this was because she was letting me. One shift in her phase and I'd be clutching at nothing. She could vanish from my grasp, sink through the dirt, or take off through the brush like a startled deer. And I'd never catch her. I'd barely managed to keep up when she raced along the river—full of hope, chasing a lie.

Back on the main roads, the first night got chilly. It was quite difficult to make a fire while holding onto her with one arm, but I managed. I clutched her close against my chest, her bony arms wrapped tight around my neck, as I bent awkwardly to clear the flattest patch of earth I could find. The flint took longer than usual. My strikes were off-angle, the sparks half-hearted, but the kindling eventually caught. The flame fluttered and I fed it gently, one twig at a time, trying not to jostle her.

Once the fire was steady, I laid out her blanket beside it. I crouched beside the fire with her still hanging from my side and, with my free hand, rigged up what little food I could spare over the flames. The smell of heat on dried rations filled the air, meager fare, but warm.

For the first time since we'd left the veil, she stirred. Like wax melting, she oozed off of me. She didn't speak. Just slid down to the blanket, her limbs folding in on themselves as she sat near the fire. A moment later, a flicker crossed her face, so slight I almost missed it. The faintest, barely-detectable upward curl of her lips.

That ghost of a smile landed harder than any ship run aground in a storm. It made the loss of her weight from my arms feel like less of a defeat. Maybe even a small victory.

I stayed vigilant. I wasn't about to let some curious coyote steal this small, fragile peace we'd reclaimed. I wouldn't let the world hurt her again, especially not now. Not while she was healing.

When dawn came, and the threat of night predators had passed, I reached for my ink and cloth. I unfolded a strip from around my neck—one of the few not yet stained with scripture—and carefully traced the symbol that had once marked her forehead. The one still carved mockingly into the obelisk beside the veil. It was burned into my memory as surely as her cries had been. The name that the sun had once remembered her by.

I waited for the ink to dry, holding the cloth in my lap like it might shatter. Then I tied it back around my throat, turned inward, hidden. A mark of reverence, to remember. Quiet and unseen. I didn't want her to look up and see it. Some wounds need time to stay closed.

The next few days passed in quiet procession. Luna stayed mostly to herself, speaking little, her words as sparse as the rations left in my bag. Every now and again she'd glance up at me, raise her arms without a word, and I'd lift her without asking questions.

The road consumed supplies faster than I would've liked. I remembered a lake not far from one of the main roads, a place I'd passed once before without much thought. It seemed as good a place as any to veer toward, if not for food, then at least for clean water and a short reprieve.

We reached the lake later than I'd expected. Luna lagged, dragging her feet, but I didn't rush her. If she needed slowness, she could have it. The sun had begun its descent by the time we arrived, smearing streaks of amber and lavender across the sky.

The surface of the lake didn't so much as twitch. No insects skimming the edges. No breeze to shift the reeds. Just a perfect stillness, so complete it felt like we'd stepped into a painting. Luna stood beside me, eyes locked on her reflection. She raised one hand, slowly tracing the space above her brows. The mark that had once glowed so brightly—her name—now gone without a trace. Her fingers moved like she could still feel it there. She was on the verge of tears. I couldn't let her fall into them.

"Hey," I said gently. "Watch this."

I peeled back the wrap from one of my fingertips, letting the golden light shine bright. Then I bent down, stuck it into the water, and wiggled it like bait. For a moment, nothing. Then a ripple, small and sudden, betrayed the presence of something beneath. A curious shape darted up. A sizable fish, too good to be true. I waited. It circled, then lunged, clamping down on the glowing lure. I lifted it free from the glassy lake.

Luna lit up. Her sadness vanished. She hopped, clapped her hands together, laughed with a kind of joy that made all the miles worth it.

"Wanna hold it?" I asked.

She nodded, holding out her small hands.

I passed the fish off to her. She squinted at it, her eyes beginning to glow again, pink like the early edges of dawn. Then the fish, uncooperative thing, started thrashing. It wriggled in her grip, tail slapping wildly, and she gasped. Her fingers sprang open like she'd been stung. The fish lifted into the air, flailing.

Her eyes snapped wide in fear. A red beam shot out. Pure and vicious. It caught the fish mid-air, turning the helpless creature to ash. No noise. Just the dull sound of powder collapsing into a neat, undisturbed pile.

The light vanished.

She stood there, hands still turned upward, blinking repeatedly as the glow dimmed from her eyes. Then the devastation set in.

She crouched beside the ashes, touched them gently, like she was checking for warmth. Her lips moved, whispering apologies the fish would never hear. Over and over, she stirred through the fine, gray dust, looking for something salvageable. There was nothing left.

I extended a hand, trying to bridge the distance, to tell her she was okay. My fingers barely touched her shoulder before she pulled away, slinking from my reach like a wounded thing too used to being struck.

The tension broke as her tattoos lit up, every single one. A surge of red pulsed through her skin in unison, flashing like a warning flare in the night. On and off again. That was all it took.

She screamed and collapsed to her knees, clawing at her arms, her chest, her sides, anywhere the cursed brands had touched her. The faint, sickly hint of burnt flesh caught in my nose.

What kind of monster would do this to someone? What sin could she have possibly committed, in her broken little body, to deserve this?

Her tiny voice cracked through the still air, raw and fractured.

"I'm sorry..."

I didn't know who she was apologizing to. Me? Herself? The fish? Her parents? Whoever it was, they weren't answering.

The last of the sun's glow drained from the sky, leaving behind the pallor of a world unsure whether to perish or suffer. She fell over and trembled against the earth, curled like a leaf that hadn't quite dropped off the tree. I moved closer, laying her blanket beside her without a word. Her heel lashed out weakly, kicking it away like a wounded rabbit using the last of its strength to deter a fox from bringing its jaws in again. She must have been shivering from the pain, not the cold. Heat was probably the last thing she wanted right now.

I stepped back, distancing myself so she wouldn't feel smothered. Then I turned to the lake.

Kneeling at the edge, I unwound the long, blood-stiffened wraps from my arms, letting them pool beside me in a muted pile. Kirtana's bindings. That thought dug in deeper than I expected. They had been hers, proof of her vow, her faith, her sacrifice. But Tristessa had cast them off. Left them behind. I had picked them up. Chosen to carry what she could not. I supposed that made them mine.

The lake's surface offered no protest. No ripples, no breeze, no motion beneath. I dipped the wraps into the cold water, rubbing the fabric between my fingers, trying to soften the dark, rusted patches into pliant linen again. Script ran along their length, hidden under the dried blood. The last piece of my sister that still existed.

As I scrubbed, the phrase began to re-emerge. The one that had burned into my brain as I tried to save her:

"Make a joyful noise unto the stars, that they might remember we were here."

I stared up at the sky, the first pinpricks of light peeking through the violet dome above. Shining. Indifferent.

Behind me, Luna's small body shuddered with sobs and coughs, pain escaping in fractured pieces. I tried not to listen, but there's a limit to how many times one can wince before it becomes habit.

I sighed. I would try again.

My voice cracked as it left me. Rough and uneven, like boots dragging across stone, but I sang anyway. Not well, though less horrifically than before. I may have inherited Kirtana's verses, but my voice was not like hers. The words still lived in me, however unfit I was to bear them. The same tune that had calmed Luna in the woods now tumbled out across the lake.

But this time, she didn't still. She didn't quiet. She didn't come to me. She didn't even look up. The verses landed with no more weight than leaves on a closed door.

I wrung out the wrappings, forever stained by my inadequacies, but legible once more. I pulled and tied them back around my arms, and sought to try something else.

A small fire sparked to life beneath my flint, the flames just enough to cook, not enough to reach her. I caught another fish, easy as the first. It sizzled over the fire while Luna lay in the dark, motionless save for the occasional shudder or pained cough. The sound of her suffering stretched the night thinner than silence ever could.

Those marks on her skin had pulsed just for an instant. A flicker. And yet here she was, nearly half an hour later, curled up on the grass, still whimpering through clenched teeth.

I remembered the alleyway. How long must she have suffered that night? The marks flared for longer then—an entire minute before she disappeared, maybe more after, singeing even the stone. I'd thought she ran because she was afraid. Now I realized she probably wanted to be alone to survive the pain.

What kind of cruelty is that?

She was a *child.* What could possibly justify this kind of punishment? Branding her twenty times or more. Each one a sentence of agony with no warning. No mercy.

And still, they weren't enough. They hadn't stopped her power. Not the petrifying gaze. Not the beam of unmaking.

The petrification—at least that had precedent. Lamias were whispered about in old Tormite records. Their venomous stares, their cursed gazes.

But that other beam. The red one.

I'd never heard of any creature, any myth, any curse that could wield that kind of power.

I looked at the bindings across her arms and legs, her face. All those brands. And none of them stopped it.

So what *were* they holding back? What greater horror were the elves afraid of her unleashing? What were they meant to prevent?

A tremor ran through me.

She hadn't screamed when the beam came. The brands hadn't ignited until the light vanished. If the brands weren't meant to *prevent* her from using her powers... was the pain only a deterrent?

She didn't seem to have any control over her abilities. If the bindings weren't preventative—they were punishment. For simply being what she was.

My gut twisted.

I looked at her, twitching in the dirt, and felt the helplessness rise again. There had to be something I could do. Someone I could find. A way to purge those marks from her skin. Would that stop the pain? Or would it unleash something even worse? Something those brands *were* holding at bay?

What if this was only a fraction of what she could do?

She whimpered, soft and broken, and the fear scattered like smoke. Whatever the truth was, whatever the danger—none of it mattered. I had to help her. Even if I didn't yet know how.

But until then, I was useless. Just another witness to her torment.

I sat cross-legged by the fire, my back aching from holding still too long. The fish hissed and spat where the skin met the flame. I tried to fan and waft the scent in her direction, hoping it might coax her out of her despair.

The full moon was rising, pale and unblinking, casting its silvery judgment over the lake. The reflection of it spread across the still water like a polished coin, unwavering, too perfect. It made our being here feel even more wrong by contrast.

The scent of char and crisped meat eventually overpowered her. She pushed herself up from the dirt with a groan, clutching the blanket like a second skin, dragging it across the short stretch of grass to the fire. She sank quietly beside the flame and folded the fabric around herself.

I offered the spit, lifting it slightly toward her and muttering a warning that it was still hot. She took it without meeting my eyes, gave it one quick breath, then sank her teeth into the fillet. I froze. My gaze didn't follow the meat, but her mouth.

They were sharp. Her teeth. I told myself it was the shadows, the fire, the angle. But by the second bite, the denial began to waver.

She took a third bite. That ended the debate. They *were* sharp, and I was absolutely certain they had not always been that way. Each one a jagged dagger, the kind of maw designed for tearing.

My eyes tilted upward. The flames danced in her irises, or perhaps they just looked redder now. Darker. I wanted to say it was a trick of the light. I wanted to believe the child next to me was unchanged. But if I'd learned anything on this road, it was that belief didn't stop anything. It just made it harder to see.

14 - Proof Enough

A few more days passed. The road stretched long and uneventful, though each mile seemed to steal another piece of her. She trudged beside me, head bowed, arms limp. She refused most of what little food we had left, but I never stopped asking. Her frame had become a painted skeleton, skin clinging to bone like she'd been sketched rather than born.

She never raised her arms to be carried. She never once said she was tired. But she was. Gods, she was.

Sleep had become foreign to her. She told me her tattoos hurt too much. I believed her. I'd seen the way her body tensed and jerked when she thought I wasn't looking, how she clutched at her arms or stomach when the pain flared up. Whatever those brands were meant to suppress, they were failing. Or maybe succeeding too well. I couldn't tell which.

When other travelers passed us—a lone rider here, a pair of merchants there—she would vanish behind me. She'd curl behind my legs, clutching my cloak, pressing her face into the folds. Like being seen had become a crime.

I didn't stop to greet them. Didn't draw their gaze. I just kept walking. She could hide behind me as long as she needed.

Our detour to the lake had altered our return path, and we came upon Boeth without fanfare. That tiny murmur of a village, nestled just where the hills began to rise, where we'd stopped after I first met her. It had felt a little brighter then. She didn't notice. Or didn't want to. Her eyes never lifted from the ground. Even the curious tilt of her ears seemed dulled.

Now, in the full light of day, with the sun casting no shadow of rain or wind, the place was still. Not in the way of peace, but of absence. A silence that pressed into your ears and made you doubt your own footfalls. No children, no livestock, no clatter of pans or idle gossip. Just shuttered windows and closed doors. Boeth was small, but there were at least a dozen homes. I found it strange that there were no signs of life this late in the day.

There was no need to stop. Her refusal to eat had left us with enough to see Rarek again. Even if we'd needed provisions, Boeth could hardly be called a trading post on a good day. Still, her feet followed mine, as they always did. So I veered left, up the gentle slope.

I wanted to see the chapel again. Just once more. It was foolish, maybe, but I needed to know if it still stood.

The hill crested like a held breath, and when I reached its peak...

The chapel was gone.

Its body lay across the grass in broken pieces. Where walls once offered shelter, there was only debris. Where prayer had once echoed, silence now reigned. And at the center of it all, the old symbol of Torm's kin. A broken hand, no longer encircled by the thorny laurel. Mercy no longer bound to resolve. Its pieces lay cracked and gutted among the wreckage. A desecrated monument to something no one believed in anymore.

I descended slowly, Luna trailing in my wake like a ghost tethered to my footprints. Mortar dust clung to everything, thick and dry. None of the newly exposed stone showed signs of age, no dark streaks from rain, no moss along the edges. This had happened recently.

I knelt by the shattered emblem. Its center was split inward, as though struck by something heavy. All around, the stones bore the same scars: bludgeoning wounds. It had been pulled down. Violently.

It hadn't been enough to simply abandon the chapel. They'd erased it.

A call rose from beyond the hill. "You there, what are you doing?"

Six soldiers crested the rise, clad in the red and gold of the capital, their posture alert but weapons undrawn. Luna immediately ducked behind me, vanishing into the folds of my cloak.

They approached with measured steps, the leader's eyes sweeping the rubble before settling on me. "What's your business here?"

I kept my voice calm. "We're just passing through. On our way back to Rarek."

"We?" he asked, brow raised. His gaze dipped, catching the subtle movements of Luna behind my legs. He squinted, judging her. "A rather curious looking creature."

He looked back up at me. "And what is your business in the capital?"

"We live there."

"You do?" he said, eyes turning to Luna again. "Where, in the gutters?"

The other soldiers chuckled at that.

I didn't rise to it. "My sister and I tend the chapel."

"The new one?"

New one? I had no idea what he was referring to. "The one in the old square."

"Ah, a Tormite," he said with disdain. "I thought you looked familiar."

One of them stepped forward, hands clasped behind his back, the swagger in his stride as heavy as the sneer on his lips. "Didn't know the cloth-skins were raising kids." He looked me up and down, then aimed a glance toward my cloak. "But I suppose with elves, you never really know which ones belong to who."

I felt the shift of Luna's weight press tighter against my leg, and there was a flicker of magenta light beneath the fabric.

Another soldier stiffened, pointing a trembling finger. "W-what was that? Was that—magic?"

"Y-yeah! She's got them marks on her skin! The ones the guild puts on crazy-folk!"

Another stepped forward. "Hand over the sorcerer."

I didn't move. "I will do no such thing."

The leader narrowed his eyes. "We've got orders to apprehend anyone suspicious headed for the capital. An apostate hiding behind a cultist is proof enough for me."

My light strengthened, beating into the back of my wrappings like a summer sun. "She's a *child*, not some ward of the state. Stand down."

I didn't shout, but the intensity in my voice, paired with the glare of light brightening across their faces, was enough to transmute their fear into self-righteous anger. Two of the soldiers reached for their blades.

And the stillness of the hill shattered.

They moved fast once the swords were drawn, emboldened by numbers and the weight of authority. One grabbed for my arm, and I twisted, catching his wrist and yanking him forward, using his momentum to sweep his legs out from under him. He fell hard, the wind knocked from his lungs. Another lunged from behind, trying to seize Luna, but I turned, elbow raised, catching him square in the ribs.

It barely phased him, the steel plate undented and unbothered. A third soldier wrapped both arms around my chest, pinning mine to my sides, while a fourth slammed the hilt of his sword into the back of my knees. I dropped to the dirt, still struggling to twist free. Luna screamed, her voice thin and brittle with panic.

A fifth soldier pressed his sword to my throat. I froze.

I felt it before I saw it. A wrongness in the air. The cold shooting down my back. The sixth had her, both hands on her tiny arms as she kicked and squirmed, her breathing clipped and rapid. Her eyes darted, then froze wide open. Her brands pulsed a deep red.

"Luna, calm down!"

A fist crashed into my gut, driving the breath from me. "Quiet," barked the one with the blade to my neck.

The leader stepped forward slowly, watching Luna with a smile that made my stomach twist, like she was a beast in a cage he already owned.

She writhed harder, her head whipping side to side, eyes starting to burn. The glow intensified—pink shifting toward violet, then to red. The heat of her markings rose like steam from a covered pot.

The light from the sun dimmed. Her eyes locked on him.

"LUNA!"

Too late.

The scream tore from her throat like a lightning strike—primal, agonized, unrelenting. And then the light came.

Beams of pure, shifting magic burst from her eyes, casting wild, searing cones that arced and lashed through the air as her head jerked and flailed.

Magenta. Red. Gray. Pale green. Each color carried a different curse, a different horror, and each found its mark.

The leader took the brunt.

The pink hit first. One hand, raised to shield his eyes, froze mid-motion, its color draining until it calcified completely, a stone effigy latched to the end of a quivering limb.

Then came the red. His breastplate crumbled. The metal shriveled like paper to flame, and the flesh beneath followed suit, flaking away into dust that drifted away on the wind.

His scream twisted with the magic, but it didn't stop.

Gray light sliced across his face, and his muscles locked, his features frozen mid-howl. Eyes wide. Mouth agape. As if he were frozen solid inside his own skin.

And then the pale green found him.

Where it touched, his skin blackened, sloughed away like rot peeling from a corpse. Patches of muscle melted. Bone emerged in places, gleaming briefly before collapsing under his weight. One leg gave out, then the other. A hand fell free. Still his body tried to scream, lips unable to loose sound as parts of him disintegrated, calcified, froze, and rotted—all at once.

Luna screamed with him, her cry fraying into something inhuman as her head swung uncontrollably. The light followed wherever she looked, scorching trails across the ground.

They threw me down like dead weight. Most of them were more eager to put distance between themselves and the beacon of chaos than to keep me subdued. The rest moved towards her, like moths drawn to a flame. I caught myself on the heel of one hand, grit biting into the linen around my palm. A moment later, the ones nearest Luna realized their mistake.

The soldier who had been gripping her wrists cried out, stumbling back as smoke rose from his gloves. The thick leather caught fire, searing the sausages inside. The bindings on her arms pulsed red-hot, angry veins of magic surging beneath her skin like molten ore. He turned to run. So did the others.

But the light caught them.

Her eyes blazed, tracking movement with terrifying precision. The beam carved after the first man's legs—a slice of red catching the backs of his calves. He didn't even scream. One step turned to ash. He stumbled, then the rest of him fell silently into the unmaking scarlet.

Another was halfway into the trees when the gray light pinned him. He froze mid-step, locked in a runner's stance, one foot off the ground, sword halfway drawn. Not a statue—just stopped. Caught in time, helpless and screaming behind unmoving lips.

Two more tried veering apart to split her aim. Her gaze swept once, twice. One turned to stone mid-sprint. The other caught a wave of green across his back and fell apart, armor pulling chunks of flesh away from each other.

All around her, soldiers were dismembered, transformed, or annihilated—and she stood at the center of it, wailing, her small frame heaving, convulsing with every ounce of power it couldn't contain.

I surged to my feet, calling out over the maelstrom.

"Luna!"

A mistake.

She stopped screaming, but her head snapped toward me like a blade unsheathed. The pale green light caught me full in the chest before I could flinch. Pain twisted, but it didn't eat through me like it had the others. I wasn't made of flesh. Still, it wracked through the scripture, whispering rot to verses that could not decay. I staggered forward.

"LUNA!"

Her eyes dropped. The light shifted, turning to gray. My body locked. The steps I had queued up dissolved. I couldn't feel my legs. Couldn't even remember how they moved.

"Luna..." I managed. Softer this time. Desperate.

Her head tilted up. The beam began to bleed at the edges.

I had no choice.

Just like Eryndra had done at the fountain, I wrenched the wrappings from my face, the fabric screaming in my ears as it tore away. My own light surged forth—a pure, searing beam, straight into her face.

She shrieked and recoiled, hands flying to her eyes as they snapped shut. Her tattoos flared white, and she toppled backward into the grass. Where she landed, the blades hissed and curled, burned black by the heat radiating off her skin.

The midday sun returned to the sky.

Half an hour crawled by, each second crushing. She lay there trembling in the scorched patch of earth.

I couldn't look away. Couldn't speak through the guilt. My legs still refused to listen, bound by the last shade of her gaze. The stillness wasn't just physical, it had rooted itself into my gut. I didn't deserve to move.

She gasped quietly, as if her body had remembered how to breathe but hadn't found the rhythm again. Her limbs twitched as she attempted to weep, but she was dry. Emptied.

"Luna?" My voice cracked.

Her ears flicked. She sat up in a heartbeat, head snapping to the sound, her pale eyes round and aimless. "Mr. Daelon?" she answered, looking vaguely in my direction. "Are you hurt?"

My chest wrenched. It would've been kinder if she'd cursed me. How she could be more concerned for me than herself was a mystery.

"I can't get to you," I said. "My legs won't move."

She crawled toward me, hands sweeping blindly through the grass. When her fingers brushed my feet, she paused, then carefully moved her hands along my shins. I couldn't feel the contact, just the weight in my chest watching her do it.

She whispered an apology, though I caught a strange lift in her voice. Relief? Her lips moved again, stringing together sounds I didn't recognize. Her hands settled firmly on my legs, and a faint prickle broke through the numbness. It started in my toes and crept upward like thawing frost. My legs twitched. Feeling returned with a thousand little needles.

"You didn't get the bad ones," she said, almost like she was speaking to herself. "I can fix this…"

And she did. My body rejoined itself.

I dropped down to my knees. "Are you okay?"

"Everything hurts. I can't see. And I'm scared."

She clutched at me and I pulled her close.

When we parted, she wiped at her eyes with the back of her hand. I caught the glint of something new: long, curved nails, sharp as thorns. Talons like an animal.

Her tail, always restless when she was upset, thrashed like a struck wire. So fast I could have swore there were two. I glanced down. One of them stilled in the dirt, twitching faintly. I counted again. Three. Two new tails, just like the first, flicking behind her.

All the questions swarmed my mind again, none of them with the answers I wanted. What was happening to her? Was this the "condition" that gatekeeper had referred to? Was it escalating?

Before I could spiral any further, she pulled me back with a question.

"Did anyone else make it?"

I scanned the remnants. Burnt shapes, piles of ash, petrified torsos with no limbs. Only one figure remained whole, frozen mid-stride near the edge of the trees, his back to us. Unmoving, but intact.

I considered lying. It would've been easy. A quick tug on her hand, a gentle word, and we could've left. Pretend there was nothing left to see, no one left to save. What would he do if she managed to revive him? Would he fight, or keep running? Who would he tell? Would anyone believe him?

I hesitated, and in that pause she pressed.

"I'm pretty sure I can fix one of them."

I sighed. Not quite defeat. Just resignation. I closed my fingers around her small hand and gave it a little squeeze.

"Come on," I said. And we walked toward the only shadow that still resembled a man.

I guided her gently to the treeline. The man's body still stood, his armor catching the sunlight with an unnatural stillness. A man locked in the final moment of terror, muscles frozen in escape, face twisted with the truth he'd never outrun. I pressed her hand to his leg, guiding her slowly. She hesitated, but began her chant.

As her fingers moved, the stiffness began to unravel. I watched the tension melt from his rigid limbs, relaxing as his body forgot the last thing it had witnessed. And then he crumpled.

She gasped as he fell. She dropped to her knees, hands scrambling across his chest. She shook him. "Wake up," her voice cracked. "Please, you're okay now."

I knelt beside her, one glance enough to tell me everything. No breath. No movement. I reached for his neck, pressed two fingers against the skin beneath his jaw. No pulse.

She kept shaking him, insisting with whispers, with gasps, with desperate little tugs on his vest. But I could feel the moment it reached her. The stillness. The silence.

Her hands slowed. Then stopped. She just knelt there, as if her body didn't know what else to do. As if letting go would mean accepting it.

Her fingers slackened as the sobs took over. Tears spilled down a face too young to know this much loss. Her shoulders trembled with each breath, her tiny frame folding further in on itself.

I slipped my hands beneath her and lifted her away. She didn't resist. Just hung over my arms like a tattered cloak, limp and frayed.

I turned toward Rarek, the chapel, my sister... whatever hope might still await us. The shattered sun hung behind, casting long shadows over the bloodless battlefield. I didn't look back.

By Torm's mercy, if it still meant anything at all, let her find some peace there. Even if it couldn't be in her heart.

15 - The Monster Within

I only got to carry her for a few hours before she demanded to be released. Her legs wobbled a bit as I set her down, but she shrugged off the contact like it stung. She didn't say thank you. Just crossed her arms, pressed her lips into a pout, and marched forward. Her ears twitched at every stray noise: the wind stirring the grass, a bird hopping between branches, my footsteps crunching behind her. Her eyes, still milky and stripped of color, betrayed her as she tripped and stumbled over every divot and stone in the road.

She refused my hand when I tried to take hers. Turned her shoulder like an infant dodging a spoonful of something it didn't like.

"What's wrong?" I asked.

She didn't answer right away. Her little fists curled tighter beside her. "I'm punishing you," she muttered, like it should've been obvious.

I blinked, but kept my confusion buried. "Punishing me?"

She nodded, once, hard. "I know I'm in trouble. For hurting people. Even if I didn't mean to. But you should be in trouble too." She sniffled, more indignation than sorrow.

"What did I do?"

"You hurt me." she said. "I can't see. Your light did that. Again. You said not to look that first time, and I listened. But then you *made* me look. You did it on purpose." Her face tightened, nose wrinkling, brows furrowed, the very image of righteous grievance.

I tried to find words, but they snagged on my guilt.

She stopped in the middle of the road, arms still folded, lips pursed. Her head turned, glaring grumpily in the wrong direction.

"Promise," she said.

"What?"

"Promise you'll never hurt me again."

I swallowed. The weight of it caught me square in the chest. All the bruises on my conscience flared anew. I wanted to say I was trying to protect her. Protect myself. That I had no choice. That if I hadn't acted, she could have…

But all that mattered to her was that it had been me. That when she was scared, it was me who'd burned her world out of sight.

"I promise."

She didn't say a word as she let me take her hand. Her clawed fingers curled tightly into mine with a desperate kind of trust. Her grip hurt, but I didn't flinch. It was better than distance.

By the time Rarek's gates crept into view, the sun had begun its slow retreat behind the crags to the west. The sky had gone to bruises, amber folding into plum. The clouds lit from beneath like a hearth fire deciding to die. The city's open gates bore their pristine, untouched, deceptive, luster. Still unsieged, at least from the outside.

We crossed the threshold as weary travelers do: slow, unannounced, unmolested by the guards who leaned in shadowed alcoves with disinterest. And yet we were seen.

A man stepped out from behind a stall and shoved me hard in the shoulder. "You think you can just walk in here?"

Luna tightened her grip on my hand, blind to the details, but not the tension. I didn't move.

A guard nearby exhaled loudly. "That's enough," he said with a half-hearted wave of his hand.

The man stared a moment longer, then turned away, muttering something I didn't care to catch.

I turned to thank the guard, but he just rolled his eyes. "You two start brawling, I gotta separate you. And I'm not in the mood."

We avoided the main road. I knew better. Cut through alleys and side paths, where the shadows lay thicker and the buildings leaned close. Doors clicked shut as we neared. Windows became eyes, narrow and gleaming. A man sharpening a blade angled it toward the street so the flash would catch my eye. Somewhere behind us, a glass bottle shattered.

The whole city felt coiled. As if every plank of wood, every bolt of iron, was waiting for some unseen signal to shatter into chaos. The air bristled with sharpened silence. A certainly-not-blessed hush. The kind of quiet that follows heresy, or heralds war.

I glanced down at Luna. The faintest shade of pink had started to return to her eyes. She blinked, pinprick pupils occasionally tracking a large object as we went by. Her vision was starting to come back, but it was clear by her puzzled squints that everything was still blurry.

We pressed on. Toward the chapel. I froze as the echo of a voice broke through the tension.

"I said back to your homes! Disperse! This is your last warning!"

Eryndra.

Even with the distance and the distortion of stone and alley, I'd know that voice anywhere. Steel in it. Duty. The kind that could drive a stake into the earth and tether the wind itself.

The blur of the crowd answered. A howl of defiance, anger, frustration. Then came the clang of metal, the true last warning. The choking scent of pitch reached me. My stomach turned. Torch smoke. Raised voices. The envoys of looming conflict.

We rounded the corner and the scene struck me. A line of guards, Eryndra among them, stood fast before the chapel, backs straight, arms drawn. Before them churned a sea of bodies, shoulder to shoulder, torch-wielding and blade-bearing, their anger so palpable it seemed to leech into the stone beneath their feet. A perfect ring of space held the crowd at bay, a no-man's-land of dread. One errant spark would break this standstill.

Unfortunately, I was that spark.

Heads turned. Torchlight danced across their wild eyes as they twisted to face me.

"There's another one!"
"They have us surrounded!"

"Every man for himself!"
"Get them!"

The shouts fanned the spark into inferno. Chaos blazed open.

Luna's fingers slid from mine. She stumbled back, blind, ears twitching madly as the tide of two dozen boots rushed toward us. I stepped between them. Dropped my shoulder and braced.

I would not let them pass.

Behind the mob, Eryndra and the guard line surged forward, meeting riot with ringmail, pig iron with steel. They fought with precision and purpose.

And I, without armor, without weapon, stood alone against twelve men driven mad by fear, fury, and the scent of blood.

They came like floodwater—shouting, blades up, fire flashing in the whites of their eyes. I dropped low, caught the first by his waist as he lunged. Momentum folded him over my shoulder and into the road behind me with a thud. My other arm caught a second man's frantic strike against my side. Not the edge of the blade, thank Torm, just the flat. I grabbed his jerkin and swept his shaking legs out from under him.

But there were too many. They didn't come in turns. They swarmed. A boot found my shin. An elbow caught my temple. One sword slid across my chest. I gritted down the pain and surged forward again, fists swinging wide.

I wasn't fighting to win. I was fighting to slow them. Fighting to block their path to her.

Luna's tiny feet shuffled behind me, unsure whether to run, and to where. I heard them, pattering against stone in hesitation and terror, and it stoked something in me hotter than the torches these men bore.

A scream of defiance rose at the edge of my throat. I let it out as I drove my palm into another attacker's chin, sending him tumbling.

I was outnumbered, outmatched, and breaking, but I stood.

Until I couldn't.

A tide of fists and boots and blades bore down on my frame, knocking me to the stone. Hands clutched at my arms, at my wrappings, dragging me backwards, deeper into the frenzy. A dagger caught my side. Another glinted and struck lower. Linen split. Blood warmed my ribs.

The torches licked closer, a half dozen flames flickering in the corner of my eye. Someone tried to light me with one, as if I were a thatch roof. The cloth resisted. I thrashed, trying to keep upright, to find purchase, but the crowd drowned me. I was pressed beneath them. Pinned by pain.

Somewhere behind me, faint but cutting through the din:

"Mr. Daelon?"

I tried to lift my head. Tried to catch a glimpse of her, searching helplessly for me.

"Where are you? Are you okay? Do you need help?"

Another blade found its mark, deep in my thigh. My own scream punched through my clenched teeth.

"M-Mr. Daelon?" Her voice trembled. So close. I couldn't see her. But she had moved nearer. Too near.

Why hadn't she run? She could've slipped through the walls, disappeared into the alleys, flown like smoke. But she didn't. I knew why.

She couldn't see. Could only listen to the cacophony of hate and fire and flesh tearing in real time.

"Run!" I choked out between coughs. "Luna, *run!*"

But her footsteps didn't retreat, they approached. I caught the flick of her tiny hands swinging wide into the storm of limbs and metal.

"Leave him *alone!*" she screamed, voice breaking into a sob.

A grunt nearby. A man's elbow dropped hard into something beside me. A soft, high squeal followed.

Another man's voice: "AHH! She *bit* me!"

A growl followed, primal and snapping, too guttural for a child. Another shout, more frightened than angry this time.

"She's a demon! Got claws and skin made of fire!"

A jagged pain cleaved through my shoulder, a blade buried to the hilt. I couldn't get off my back. The world spun. I saw one man cock back and kick. A sickening thump. Another of her squeaks, lower now.

The sunlight faded suddenly. Too early for sunset. The sky drank its own brilliance, swallowing it all at once for the second time that day.

"No—LUNA, *DON'T!*"

She didn't listen.

The air split with the howl of unmaking.

Where once there were cheers and jeers, now there was only the primal, piercing shrieks of the undone. The chaos turned. The bravado of the crowd evaporated. Gone was the amber light of torches, replaced by ribbons of searing magic slashing reality in twain.

That sickening red raked through the mob. Arms detached from shoulders, torsos fell from hips. Black ash and cinders swirled through the air like a blizzard attending a funeral. The scent of burning flesh came first, but then came worse.

When the pink carved back above me, I heard the crack of stone—arms turned statues, faces frozen mid-shout. Limestone sculptures of hands and heads hit the cobbles around me, shattering into jagged pebbles.

The pale green sliced across the square next, and the smell of rot overtook everything as the living turned to week-old corpses.

Then came the stilling gray. One man's scream cut off mid-note, teeth bared, eyes wide. Blades and torches caught mid-swing extinguished, as if time itself had frozen.

The ground beneath me slicked with blood and ash, I dragged myself forward, inching toward the cyclone of magic that was Luna. She stood at the eye of her own storm, arms slack at her sides, head flinging from side to side with wild, blind panic. The beams lashed out with her gaze, painting the square in ruin.

I called to her softly, steady, desperate. Told her I was here, told her she was safe. Begged her to stop. But her eyes remained wide, pouring their terrible radiance into a world she could barely see.

Around us, the crowd of bystanders had scattered, the instinct for survival overtaking whatever hatred or curiosity had drawn them here. I saw them scramble over one another, some turned to statues mid-climb, others crumbed into heaps of soot as the light caught them. Friend, foe, or neutral, no one was safe from the carnage.

Only Eryndra remained. Stubborn and resolute, she stood a dozen paces off, most of her guard already reduced to mangled pieces strewn between us. Her teeth clenched as she tried to move, but her legs refused her. She must have gotten caught in the gray, paralyzed from the knee down just as I had been. She wasn't going anywhere. She didn't flinch when the red seared across the square again, she ducked, just barely. The band of nothing missed her by inches, slicing a clean void into the side of a building beside her.

"Daelon, do something!" she screamed.

I reached for Luna's hand—nothing. My fingers passed through her like smoke. No weight, no heat, just the shimmer of untouchable light. Her brands were erupting now, nearly blinding in their intensity. Not just glowing, but lifting, bulging outward as they throbbed with a heartbeat of their own. Her skin blistered around them, yet she didn't seem to notice. Or couldn't.

Another twist of her neck, another beam of pink cut low. Eryndra raised her shield just in time, only for the iron slab to seize and calcify in her grip. She clung to her last line of defense like a broken gravestone.

I kept my voice low, steady, trying not to let the horror take root in my throat. Luna couldn't see. Terror fixed on her face, lashing out with the only thing she had left. And I couldn't even touch her.

So I started humming.

The moment the melody left my throat, her ears twitched. The first sign she'd heard me, the first thread I could grasp. I leaned into it, weaving my voice around the hymn Kirtana had once loosed into this very square. A lament shaped like hope. A dirge disguised as beauty. Luna's breath, uneven and ragged, began to slow, stuttering to make the notes like her lungs didn't know whether to obey the music or the pain.

I reached for her again. Nothing. Still smoke. Still light.

But she heard me. I could see it in her jaw, clenched tight as her new, elongated teeth flashed in the sickly glow. Her fists closed and shaking, her ears swiveling wildly as if seeking a way to shut the world out. Her whole body a snare pulled taut. She was still fighting. Whether it was against my voice or the magic clawing through her veins, I couldn't say. But the war inside her was plain.

When the song shifted, the minor key rising, she staggered. Her hands flew up, not to shield her eyes this time, but to dig into her own scalp, nails raking across her temples. Her brands ignited white, unnaturally pale, their borders burning the skin around them to a cracked, smoking black. The contrast was sickening.

I moved to reach her, to stop her, to soothe her, but she jumped back, shrieking.

Her body twisted toward her left arm. She stared at it in horror, then threw herself at it, tearing at the white-hot sigil that pulsed between the bones. Her fingers clawed desperately, as if she could dig the light out with her bare hands.

Then it detonated.

A concussive burst split the square in two, heat and pressure collapsing in a blink, and Luna's arm vanished. No blood, no bone, just mist. Her body flung back, mine with it. I landed hard, a broken stone cutting into my ribs. The shockwave hit the side of the chapel, shaking its old stones loose. A wall gave out, the roof above it collapsing like brittle parchment. Rubble crashed beside me, inches from my head.

And still her eyes screamed.

She writhed, broken and bleeding, her left arm ending in a ragged stump. She grasped at it, at nothing, at the pain that must've been eating her whole.

Her voice—gods, her voice—howled through the ruins. Beyond words, a sound carved from agony itself. It scraped down the inside of my skull, threshed my thoughts to silence. The music, the song, what little I had left, died on my lips.

I couldn't reach her. I couldn't touch her.

And the rest of those damned brands... pulsed with a hideous white glow, each one a charge ready to blow. If they didn't cook her alive, they'd do what the first had done. Turn her to paste.

I didn't know what to do.

I thought back to Boeth. Noon felt a lifetime ago. I'd nearly blinded her then, and only barely stopped the storm inside her. Her eyes hadn't had time to heal. Neither had her trust. But what else could I do?

And yet, I'd made her a promise.

I told her I wouldn't hurt her again.

Now she lay broken in the square, bleeding light and sobs and the last shreds of herself—and I was hesitating. Was I really going to let her die for the sake of my word? I got to my feet, but couldn't move myself forward.

"Daelon, do it!" Eryndra's voice cut through the smoke and ruin.

I turned to her. Her eyes were locked on mine, distant across the rubble. Was she reading my thoughts?

Eryndra's voice rang out again, firm and cutting. "I can see it in your stance, Daelon! You've got something, I know it. Stop weighing the cost—we'll be dead before you finish thinking. Whatever it is, just *do it!*"

I turned back toward Luna. Her ears had perked. Her head was tilting, slow and searching, toward the sound that had broken the silence. Toward Eryndra.

The beam swinging toward her was red. Not stone. Not paralysis. Not decay. Red meant erasure. Annihilation.

Eryndra's shield came up, but that slab wouldn't save her. It would turn to dust along with her.

I yanked the cloth from around my arm, and threw forth the light.

Golden brilliance blazed from me, pouring out into the air with force enough to ripple the smoke. It met the oncoming red just feet from Eryndra's shield, the two beams crashing like dueling waves. The square lit like dawn had broken early, each color starving shadows in opposite directions.

The red pushed harder. It didn't flicker. It didn't waver. It simply advanced.

I grimaced and tore another strip of cloth from my arms, adding the light underneath its verse to the golden blaze. The beam thickened and flared, but I was still losing ground.

Luna's fury didn't pause to breathe.

My feet dug into the shattered stone beneath me as I ripped off more bindings, letting them hang loose. Each new bit of exposed flesh brightened the gold, slowing the red but only delaying the tide.

I only had one wrap left. And I was still hesitating. Still hoping she'd burn herself out. Hoping the beam would shift color. I bowed my head, praying silently and desperately, that she wouldn't make me choose.

Torm, right hand of Tyr, god of duty, courage, loyalty, and bravery... I don't know if you can hear me. I don't even know if you're real anymore. But if ever you walked beside me, if ever I was made in your image…

I choked on the next words.

I am about to betray a child. I am about to break a promise she made me swear on nothing but her trust. And she doesn't have much of that left to give.

The light grew hotter. My arms trembled. I could feel her name on the binding around my neck like it had come alive, like it knew what I was about to do.

Tell me this is right. Tell me this is mercy. Tell me I'm not damning her to save her. Give me a sign. Please.

"STOP WAITING, DAELON!" Eryndra bellowed from behind her shield.

There was nothing. Not even the lie of comfort. No voice. No wind. No righteous fury or divine lament. Just Eryndra shouting my name over the roar of colliding powers.

I thought of my promise for just a moment longer.

And then I broke it.

I pulled the cloth from around my neck, the one I'd drawn Luna's name upon, and cast out the last of the light. With every ounce of will, I stepped forward. I pressed it between us, a golden wall clashing against the blood-red surge.

The two powers collided in incandescent fury. Light and dark roared against one another, flaring hot enough to crack the cobblestones beneath us. My whole body shook as I drew strength from every place within me.

The red wave faltered. I felt it, warping away, unraveling in the face of something stronger.

Yet each step forward was its own betrayal of her. My feet, sluggish under the strain of the light's drain, felt like they were trudging through ice atop the mountain. That same dead slope. That same desperate climb. Only this time, the summit burned, and failure would mean death.

I pressed on, pouring every ounce of myself into the gold. I was faith unbound. A verse stripped bare of parchment. A truth too old to die.

When I reached her, I stood not as her friend, not as her protector, not even as a man. I was the message made manifest. Towering over her trembling, twitching frame, draped in the vestments of pure, searing light. The light of all that I was.

The red faltered. Cracked. It sputtered like a dying flame resisting the wind. And finally, it faded—defeated.

I wished it hadn't.

Because what lay beneath was worse.

Her face lifted to mine. No recognition in her gaze, just madness. Blood vessels split like lightning in her sclera, veins pulsing with power not meant for mortals. Her pupils had narrowed to reptilian slits, and her lips peeled back in a grin too wide for the child I knew.

I saw it. The demon. The specter curled inside her, clawing from beneath the veil of her skin. It grinned at me, mocking, daring me to do something. Anything. Two dozen brands flared at once, each one screaming, holding it in place by a thread and a prayer.

And then... it retreated. Curling inward like smoke retreating into a pipe. Her eyes fluttered, dimmed, and returned to their soft, haunted normal.

And in the sheen left behind, in the moisture of her exhausted, tear-slicked stare, I saw another monster.

My own reflection.

And unlike the thing inside her, this one she would remember. For it would be the last thing she ever saw.

16 - The Devil is Man

Luna fell back, kicking and screaming, her single hand pressing firmly into her eyes to scrub the pain from them. My light faded to a soft glow as I knelt by her, hands rewrapping the bindings around my chest. I tugged the wrappings around my neck, arms, and legs, feeling the weight of anonymity return. I'd forgotten how exhausting it was to be completely unmasked. The ritual was a reminder of why we hid, how we survived.

I reached out, fingertips hovering uncertainly before touching her knee. "Luna…"

She sprang to her feet with a feral intensity. Her voice cracked like flint. "Don't touch me!"

"Luna, it's me..."

"I know who you are! You smell like the dead places." She stared through me with the washed-out white voids where her eyes used to be. "I said: don't touch me!"

I froze, shards of guilt and sorrow sweeping my chest. I could feel the distance between us widening, longer and deeper than any cave, any chasm. And I realized the aftermath, the real aftermath, had only just begun.

"Luna, I'm sorry, I…"

"YOU PROMISED!" she screamed. The sound cut me worse than anything ever had. It pierced deeper than every sword.

She stood there, ash caked to her face. "You promised you wouldn't hurt me again!"

I opened my mouth, searching for something to put in it. Anything. Some explanation, some plea for understanding. "You were hurting people. You were hurting yourself. If the rest of the brands had gone off—"

"Maybe you should have just let me DIE!" she said, her voice cracking as her hand clutched at the air where her other arm used to be.

The world went very still. She was just… saying it. Like a simple fact. Her gaze was blank, her ears twitching as if listening for some answer I didn't have the strength to give.

"Luna, let's get you inside. I can see that you're hurting and—"

"At least you can still SEE!"

She turned and bolted, blindly tripping over a hunk of stone jutting from the rubble. It could've been part of a toppled column, or a piece of someone who hadn't made it out alive. I couldn't tell. She threw her arm out to break the fall, but her balance was all wrong. With only one arm to catch herself, she crumpled. Her palm struck first, then the rest of her pitched sideways and smacked hard against the unforgiving cobbles.

She lay perfectly still for a long moment. Then she started to cry. Loud, broken sobs. The kind I'd heard outside the veil when she was begging to go home. The kind that came from betrayal.

My feet locked in place. This was my fault.

She sat up slowly, shaking, and turned her face toward me with eerie precision. Her blind eyes narrowed, and her voice came low and venomous.

"Even if my eyes go back to normal, I never want to see you again."

Then, without another word, she turned and stepped through the scorched wall, vanishing into the stone.

I had broken my promise. I had saved her. And in doing both, I had lost her.

Back in the chapel, where the silence was louder than any hymn we'd ever sung, I guided Eryndra up the nave. Her stiff-legged gait scraped awkwardly across the tile. The wall to the west had collapsed inward, and a single defiant column of dust filtered down from the breach in the roof. I steadied her as we neared the altar. She winced, jaw set, every step a skirmish between will and ruin. Her feet hadn't yet relearned how to bend, but her legs were moving now, barely. It was something.

We hadn't said a word since Luna vanished. Her voice still echoed in my skull like a curse. And I could feel the weight behind Eryndra's silence too. There was a reckoning forming on her tongue. I could sense it in the way her shoulders squared, in the way her fingers kept flexing and relaxing as if sorting through a sheath of arguments she planned to draw, one by one.

The front doors flew open. Selva burst through, her cloak askew, panic stitched into the corners of her face.

"I came as soon as I heard," she gasped. "By Torm's mercy… what happened here?"

"*Someone* brought a ticking spellbomb into the city," Eryndra said. "And it went off. We were lucky it only took part of the chapel with it and not the entire district."

I met her sideways glance with a dirty look of my own. We both broke it off and looked back to Selva, clearly confused.

Eryndra continued. "*Some of us* believe every broken thing deserves shelter, even if it's already burning."

"Is it not the way of Torm to extend our mercy and kindness to those in need?" Selva asked.

Erydra grit her teeth, refusing to look at me. "I'm sure Daelon can explain it better. He's grown very... *attached*."

At her snide comment, I let go.

Eryndra pitched sideways, catching herself with a clumsy jerk of the now-stone slab she refused to relinquish. Her face twisted, tight, proud, and plainly pissed. That told me everything I needed to know. I'd hit the mark, and wounded her pride.

Selva's brows pinched together as she stepped cautiously between us, her eyes flicking from my loosened hand to Eryndra's stiffened shoulders.

"Please," she said, "we're all still living. That alone is something to thank the stars for. If my husband were still alive, he wouldn't want to hear us bickering inside the chapel."

She moved to the far side of the altar and knelt before the shrine with the same quiet reverence she always did. Her hands folded, head bowing low. "At least the heart of the chapel remains," she murmured. "Thank the light for sparing what matters."

A group of guards entered the chapel, shoulders slumping with relief as they realized the danger had passed. I recognized only one face from the assembly before the riot: a young man whose right arm had turned to stone. He met my gaze with something like an apology, his face pinched.

"Captain sent us," he said, gesturing to the man behind him.

The captain wore a crisp, unreadable expression. He stepped forward, surveying the remnants of our sanctuary without emotion. Dust drifted through the hole in the wall, illuminated by his lantern.

"People outside are blaming this on the Ethereals. Even though your man here," he nodded to the injured guard, "told them otherwise. But the crowd isn't listening. They're demanding justice."

Eryndra's jaw tightened, but it was the captain who spoke again. "Given the optics—Ethereals, magic, civilians—if you remain among our ranks, you risk provoking another riot. I can't have that."

His eyes found Eryndra's: unwavering, authoritative. "We have to dismiss you. We also suggest that you leave the city before things take a turn for the worse."

I could see layers of rage and hurt crack the hard armor of Eryndra's composure, the same armor she'd forged with years of absence from the chapel, midnight patrols, and ceaseless vigilance—all to prove that an Ethereal could stand as a protector in this rabid city.

She had sacrificed more than most would ever understand. Late-night watches that left the shrine exposed. Tending the wounded until dawn. Holding fast to the belief that her service, her presence, could bridge the gap between fear and acceptance.

Now, a scapegoat. A brutal irony that twisted her resolve into something brittle and sharp.

Her voice cut through the haze. "I won't hide or disappear so the captain can look like he's doing something. I did this for Rarek." She raised her badge, once a symbol of valor, now a cursed coin of appeasement. She ripped it free. With cruel calm, she flung it down the aisle. It clattered at his feet.

"Take it," she spat. "And go be a hero to the rabble. Sell them security through betrayal."

The crackling of torches and the shifting of men in armor kept the sacred silence of the chapel at bay. The badge, dangling in the dust of the floor, became a monument to everything Rarek had lost: faith, trust, courage.

I stayed silent, heart waging a war between pride and fear. Without her duty to anchor her, to pour herself into… how long before Rarek shattered her too?

Selva stayed planted, voice hushed but unwavering, kneeling before the shrine. "We will endure," she prayed, speaking both to the divine and to the fractured family standing before it.

The captain bent low, retrieving the badge from where it had landed. He held it a moment, perhaps weighing the gravity of the act that had just unfolded, then turned on his heel and gave a sharp nod. The guards filed out in silence, boots clicking dully against the stone.

At the threshold, he glanced back over his shoulder. "I hope you heed my warning. Take the night to pack and leave Rarek before things escalate."

Eryndra scoffed, her reply more venom than words. "Take your warning and choke on it."

He didn't look back again. The doors swung closed behind him.

Selva remained at the altar, thankfully out of earshot as Eryndra leaned in close.

"You've doomed us," she whispered. "Because of your theatrics, we've lost everything. My badge. My post. Our right to be here. To be seen. And here you are, shambling back into Rarek like your absence hasn't burned it all down."

I stared at her, half in disbelief. "I was taking care of Luna."

She swept a hand across the broken chapel, the splintered pews and scorched floor. "Look around, Daelon. That's what your care bought us. Your years of searching. Your endless trips to nowhere. Your convictions. All that for what? The square is gone. The entire city turned against us. She turned on you, blamed you, and ran."

Her voice dropped lower, almost shaking. "You left Rarek to save it. But then you left *that* path, too. For a girl you didn't know. You traded everything we built for a child who spat in your face. She doesn't want you, Daelon. And you can't fix her. All you've done is give yourself away, piece by piece… and it still wasn't enough."

I didn't answer. Couldn't.

Because she didn't know.

Didn't know what it was like to come home from the lonely wilds and be met only with scorn. To scrape for meaning in a world that met your faith with pity or contempt. To find, in the shadow of all that, a small, wounded soul who smiled up at you like you mattered. Who laughed when you tried. Who cried, and let you hold the pieces.

Luna didn't need sermons or shrines. She needed someone, *anyone*, to care for her in spite of what she was. And maybe—selfishly—so did I.

But Eryndra wouldn't understand that. She'd only hear the betrayal in it. The weight she'd borne without me. The love I never gave her. That she never gave me.

So I said nothing.

The doors groaned under the impact of torches and boots, and suddenly they were inside: a new mob. Men stormed in, torches gleaming, clubs raised, blades flashing.

Pew after pew splintered under their blows. They tore at the wood and stone with furious intent. One kicked over a vase; water and cracked pottery forming paste with the ash covering the floor.

I could only move to intercept, to push and pull, trying to disarm rather than kill, every moment a desperate gamble.

Eryndra tried valiantly to reach Selva, who stood paralyzed before the shrine. She staggered forward, legs sluggish, each step a battle, her shield raised. She swung it hard into a man who lunged for the sacred emblem. It cracked his shoulder, sending him sprawling. But she couldn't keep pace; there were too many of them.

Selva only blinked, rooted to the spot, clutching her heart like a silent prayer. I lunged between them, arms swinging wide to knock weapons aside, but soon they pressed around me too, my unarmed strikes no match for their numbers.

They yanked down sconces, tossed candlesticks, and ripped at banners. When one lunged at Selva, I kicked his chest to push him away. Another aimed for Eryndra, she planted her feet and rammed him with that damned shield, sending him crashing into the splintered pews.

Dust and smoke billowed up into the air. Shouts and whimpers echoed off the walls. I heard the cringe of timber cracking, the lick of a blaze near the altar, and creeping toward it. Our sanctuary turned battleground.

I could see through the haze that Eryndra was fighting beside me. Even partially immobilized, she swung at every intruder within reach. I followed her lead, grabbing arms, knocking foes unconscious, pleading with them to stop. They only roared back.

The fire grew. I reached for Selva's arm and pulled her behind me, but the mob circled, and a cry from her hit my spine like a lash. I spun around and saw the glint of steel jutting from her front, quivering with the force of the thrust. Her eyes were wide and glassy. The man behind her grinned, almost pleased with himself, as if murder were a trick he'd pulled off well. I didn't think. I shattered his arm with a snap that echoed louder than the surrounding chaos. He released his blade. Eryndra didn't accept it as the end; her shield cracked into his skull with a terminal crunch.

But the moment cost us. The mob had surged toward the shrine. A few haphazard, drunken strikes was all it took. The old stone cracked, groaned, then caved in on itself, the relic clattering into the rubble. The altar that had stood for centuries, our last sacred remnant of the divine, gone in seconds to rusty pig iron and cheap wood.

Eryndra screamed. A sound I'd never heard from her before. She threw the shield—not at a man, but through him. His ribcage folded, and he hit the wall without a breath left to give.

And yet the mob cheered. They screamed like they'd won something. Smoke curled up to the ruined rafters. They spilled out the broken doors, their torches trailing behind them like some procession from the hells. The chapel reeked of blood and ash. It sang with the dying fire and Selva's shallow, failing breaths.

I sank to one knee beside Selva, because I couldn't bring myself to stand while she died. Eryndra remained upright, her legs stiff and uncooperative. Selva's hands fumbled for the long strips of bandages wrapped around me, and the ones around Eryndra's legs—her final grasp for the faith that had once held us all together. She closed her eyes, breath rattling in her chest.

"May the right hand of Tyr guide and protect you," she whispered.

Then she was gone.

I looked up at Eryndra, waiting for the explosion. For a curse. A scoff. Anything.

But her face was locked in something colder. Brows slightly drawn, jaw clenched just enough to twitch. The kind of restraint that didn't come naturally to her. Not Eryndra.

She turned, slowly, her gaze sweeping over the chapel like she was appraising a battlefield. She stood, spine straight, arms loose at her sides. Too still.

"Eryndra…" I said, barely above a breath. I rose, reached for her hand, her cold fingers stiff in mine.

She didn't turn, but she softly withdrew her hand from mine. The flames painted her in red, and as they moved, the color in her eyes didn't.

My last sister had gone hollow.

Eryndra, or whoever she was now, bent stiffly at the hip, pulling at the bindings encircling her rigid legs. Selva's hands had gripped those words as she died, as if they could carry her the rest of the way. The red ethereal ripped them off and cast them aside as if the words burned now.

Her gaze turned to me, and I didn't recognize what stared back. It wasn't heat and fury, it was cold judgment. "You'd rather cradle a cursed stray and chant crumbling lines of scripture while the people you claim to serve are butchered? You still think your light is enough? That it *matters*? You stood there empty-handed while they gutted Selva. While they tore this place apart. You don't carry a blade, Daelon, because you think it makes you righteous. But the truth is, you're just too much of a coward to fight for what you claim to believe in. This is what you deserve."

She swept an arm toward the wreckage. Toward the blackened beams and shattered glass, the still-burning pews and Selva's cooling body. "This... broken shrine. The duty, the surrender. If this is what the faith is, then you can keep it. The sermons. The silence. The waiting. The *weakness.* You can hold the memory of her, and Kirtana, and everyone else you doomed by clinging to an interpretation of the word that never gave anything back."

She shoved past me, the firelight coiling along her jaw. "You live to be good, but you let everyone around you die. So keep your burden. Keep your pacifism. Keep this forsaken ruin and see how long your virtue protects it. It is a grave, Daelon. And I'll not let you bury us all in it."

She stepped away, through the licking flames that wavered and parted like they feared her. The slab of stone she'd once carried like a badge of honor lay untouched behind her. She didn't so much as glance at it, pausing only once she'd filled the doorframe. "There's nothing left here worth protecting. And if you have any brains, you'll leave. Before this city finishes what it started."

And then she was gone. Just like Tristessa. Just like everyone.

I moved through Rarek like a shadow. Eryndra's wrappings were stiff as I tied them around my legs, still faintly warm from her touch, though the red ethereal had left no parting warmth in her words. The stone shield—Eryndra's burden, now mine—hung from my back like the past itself. Damned heavy thing. But I carried it, leaving it behind felt too much like letting her go.

The streets were quiet in that accusatory way. The kind of hush that follows a beating, when everyone looks away and pretends it didn't happen. The air still stank of soot and rot. Windows were shuttered, doors barred, yet every wall I passed felt like it was watching me.

I didn't belong here anymore. Perhaps I never had.

Stetson's house lay on the edge of the old quarter, its familiar silhouette my last bastion of peace and safety. If I was going to leave Rarek, I needed direction. A lead. A thread, however thin, to pull me forward. Toward that last shrine: the one lost in no-man's land. Toward *something.*

Something to focus on.

Something to keep me from listening to the flames and ash and screams playing back endlessly in my skull, each one echoing like a bell I couldn't drown out.

I knocked. Stetson opened the door just wide enough to squint at me, the chain bolt snapping taut between us. His eyes suspicious, searching. Then they softened. Recognition. Regret. He fumbled with the latch and hurried me inside.

"Word travels," he muttered, voice low as he shut the door behind me. "Even after nightfall."

The house was darker than I remembered it. Curtains drawn. Candles snuffed. A thin layer of dust lined the corners, like even he had stopped trusting the world outside. He looked like he hadn't slept since my last visit. Whatever scraps of trust he had left, he was spending them now.

"I need everything you know about the last shrine," I said. "The one in the wastes."

He didn't question it. Just nodded. He'd been waiting for this.

He knelt beside an old cabinet and pulled it open, revealing a stash of papers, tools, a few scroll tubes, and an inkpot with no lid. His fingers worked fast, practiced. These weren't leftovers from the archive, these were the parts he'd decided were too valuable to leave behind.

He pointed to a blot of ink, circled in haste, its edges already beginning to smudge. It sat in the band of the sand-choked corridor between Rarek and Talakit. An ugly strip of no-man's land too dry for kings to claim. Too distant for laws to find you. He didn't need to say what sort of things made their homes there. Every map bore warnings, but none so honest as his grimace.

"That's where it would've been. A temple, if it was ever real."

It looked wrong on the map. Smudges and old folds conspiring to erase the place entirely. I didn't care. I needed something to chase. Something to bleed for. If it had ever stood, I would find it. And if it hadn't… then at least I'd die moving toward something that wasn't a lie.

"I don't think I'll be coming back," I said.

Stetson nodded, lips pressed thin. "I've thought of leaving myself. Plenty of times." His hand drifted around the counter, fingers tapping. "But something always kept me here. Can't name it. Can't justify it. Just is."

I didn't answer.

His brow furrowed a little, the way it did when he reread a line and found a second meaning hiding beneath it. "You mean more than the city."

I kept my eyes on the map.

Stetson let out a slow breath, long enough that the silence settled between us like dust. Then he cleared his throat—gruff, almost irritated, which meant he was trying to say something honest.

"Daelon… you've been the one steady thing in this place." His voice stayed low, as if he feared saying it too plainly. "When the rest of us bent, you didn't."

He glanced toward the drawn curtains, the city hidden beyond them. "If Rarek still has anything worth salvaging, it's because people like you walked once through it."

I didn't move.

Stetson scratched at his beard, searching for the right tone. "Whatever you find out there—temple or sand—you won't break. You're too damned stubborn." A faint huff of a laugh, quickly swallowed. "Don't let this place convince you otherwise."

He shifted his weight, suddenly uncomfortable with his own sincerity. "Just… remember someone here was glad to know you."

It was as close as he'd come to saying he'd miss me.

I offered him my thanks and turned for the door.

"Wait."

His voice had gained weight. I turned, and he was holding out an old sword, its luster dulled from years but its edge still intact. I looked to him, already bracing to decline.

His face said not to. This wasn't a suggestion. It was the bare minimum. Not just for the road ahead, but the road right outside his door. The world I was stepping back into was not the one my idealism still clung to. And he knew I wouldn't let myself see it.

I took the weapon in both hands. It felt wrong. Heavy in places it shouldn't be. But familiar, too. Like a name I hadn't spoken aloud in a decade. A verse I'd left unfinished. I hadn't forgotten how to wield it. I'd just chosen to stop.

Stetson didn't move as I tested the weight of the sword in my grip. He didn't need to. His parting words landed with the same force as the weapon he'd just given me.

"Sometimes to defend yourself from man, you have to act like one."

Not a goad. Not some drunken call to valor. Just a truth. Cold, heavy, and long ignored.

I didn't answer. But something must have shifted in my face. Something brittle enough to crack. He gave a slow, tired nod as if to say: *That's all I needed.*

I turned and stepped back into the dark. The city was quiet now. The kind of quiet that hangs before a funeral. Or after a fire. And I was carrying both.

17 - Nothing Valued Remains

The moon hung low when I slipped through the quiet streets, each footfall careful and light in the dark. Ahead, the ghaf tree's silhouette loomed, its leaves impossibly full for the season. Vale's smug words echoed in my mind: "Its leaves are said to symbolize the victory of good over evil." My hand tightened on the sword's hilt, a sudden ache of disgust twisting through me. Here was his symbol, flourishing under his lies, casting its broad canopy over the stars.

A flicker of motion near the base caught my eye. Someone, too deliberate, moving toward the colonnade by the library.

I followed quickly, keeping to the darkest edges of the street, eyes fixed on the figure ahead.

Nobody walked alone this late at night. Especially not with previous riots, the smoke, and smell of rot starting to thread its way into every alley. Whoever this was didn't seem afraid. That alone set my nerves on edge. No torch, no lantern, not even the flick of a spelllight to guide them.

A lone elf, perhaps? I doubted it. Too brazen. Steps not trying to be silent. I kept my distance, adjusting my pace to match theirs as they disappeared behind the columns of the old library's rear portico. My curiosity itched like a wound. There weren't many left in Rarek who dared the night. I needed to know who still did. Especially after today's events.

I circled wide around the library's outer wall, steps silent against the deadened street. Just enough distance, just enough light. I rounded the far end of the colonnade, and nearly collided with him.

He didn't startle. Not so much as a twitch. His eyes met mine instantly, like he'd been waiting there the whole time. The curve of his lips was warm, welcoming even, as if I were a long-lost brother returning from some noble campaign. Aurelian Vale.

"Ah, the curious ethereal," he said, voice slick as butter. Only then did it strike me: he'd never asked for my name during our last encounter. And I'd never offered it. "Is there something you need my help understanding again?"

His gaze didn't move. Not to the sword in my hand. Not to the subtle shift in my posture. I could've been holding a candlestick for all the attention he gave it.

"What are you playing at?" I asked. "First preaching Torm—wrongly—then tearing him down in the next breath. Deluding the people of Rarek, feeding their hate, bending their poverty into weapons. What is this to you? Theater? A sermon? A sales pitch?"

He didn't respond.

I stepped closer. "You walk into town dressed as a priest, quoting virtues you clearly don't understand. The next time I see you, you're dressed as a common man, claiming to work for the king. And now I find you skulking through the city like a stray, without so much as a torch to your name. Why?"

Still nothing. His smile never wavered. A big, toothy grin, like a proud parent watching their child perform a stage play.

"Are you lost? Or is this just the costume for tonight?" I asked. "Saint in the square, beggar in the dark. What's next? Tyrant at the altar?"

Aurelian's expression warmed, false reverence tucked neatly behind his smirk.

"Talakit," he said, as if savoring the name. "Is a place that loves the sound of its own voice. You won't find many starving souls there, not physically. Spiritually, though? They're famished, yet too proud to admit it."

He leaned back, resting a hand on one of the smooth columns of the colonnade, the moonlight sketching soft silver against his cheek.

"They're educated. Meticulously so. Taught to argue, to cross-examine, to spot a fallacy before you can finish your sentence. They read theory, not scripture. And when a man stands before them with conviction in his voice, they don't listen for the meaning. They listen for the flaw."

He tilted his head, eyes still locked on mine. "Every phrase you speak to them is a test. Every gesture, a calculation they'll dissect before deciding whether to laugh at you, tolerate you… or destroy you."

His smile never changed, but it no longer reached his eyes.

"They're not cruel. Just... clever. So very clever." He paused for a moment. "As you can imagine, getting any of them to join hands under a common cause, even a well-justified one, can be... *challenging.*"

Aurelian's gaze drifted past me for a moment, toward the city sprawled out in smoke and silence beneath the tree's branches. Then he stepped in closer. Intimate, like a confession whispered between old friends.

"But the people of Rarek…" he said, "are something different entirely."

He looked back at me, eyes shining with something like delight. "I see possibility. They haven't been taught to doubt every word they hear. They haven't been hardened into cynics with degrees or dogma. They haven't built their national pride around being the smartest people in the world."

He lifted a hand, gesturing broadly to the empty street. "They still believe in *things.* Simple things. Money. Tradition. Justice. They might not understand the full shape of those things, but the fire is there. All you need is the right fuel."

His fingers came together, thumb to forefinger, miming a flame catching.

"They are not burdened by knowledge, or options. They cling to what they know. Or rather... what they *think* they know. Faith, pride. They crave unity more than truth. Belonging more than clarity. Give them a banner to march behind, a villain to blame, and you will see how quickly they learn to move as one."

I narrowed my eyes at him. "Is that why you've come here? Just to turn a city on itself?"

Aurelian's grin didn't fade, it widened. "My talents," he said, as if tasting the phrase, "were not... *appreciated* in Talakit. You might say the soil there was too rocky for anything new to grow. But a smart man knows when to stop sowing in barren fields. He finds more fertile ground. Somewhere his ideas might take root."

I spat. "If your 'talents' are blasphemy and fearmongering, perhaps you should consider learning a trade."

That made him laugh. Really laugh. His head tilted back as the sound echoed through the sleeping city. It wasn't mocking, not exactly. Just... tickled. Like he was genuinely enjoying our little chat.

"A tradesman, me? Can you imagine?" Aurelian mused, holding up his scrawny arms and unblemished hands. "I've neither the body nor the background to be a laborer. But suppose I did work my hands to the bone, break my back, and sweat in the sun... what would I do it for? Satisfaction? A pitiful wage?"

I clenched my shoulders, jaw tightening. "You seem to have a taste for coin, judging by how much you were collecting in the square."

He tutted softly, wagging a finger. "Ah, no no no. That's where you're mistaken." His eyes glittered in the pale light. "I come from a very old, very well-regarded family in Talakit. I inherited more coin than these poor folk could gather in a dozen lifetimes. I don't *need* their copper."

"Then why take it?"

"Because need is the foundation of loyalty," he said, smiling. "A man with an empty belly listens more closely. A desperate mother with sick children doesn't ask as many questions. Fear is the lever that moves mountains. You show a crowd the edge of ruin, and they'll run straight off it if they think you're holding the bridge to their salvation. It's remarkably entertaining."

I grabbed Aurelian by his shirt, slamming him into the stone wall and pressing the sword against his throat. My voice trembled as I spoke.

"You desecrate Torm with this manipulation. True sacrifice is borne of conviction and preparation, of hardship faced willingly. Not something to be forced upon people to keep them in line! You have the *gall* to twist faith into fear? I should cut your tongue out, or remove your head."

His smile remained unshaken, serene even, as if my steel held no meaning for him.

"Anger is merely fear's attempt to hide," he said, voice still perfectly calm. "Tell me, Ethereal, what is it about me you fear?"

His composure, utterly unbroken, reached inside me and pulled at my own uncertainties.

"You've turned them into zealots," I hissed. "Tribalistic, bloodthirsty fools. Abandoning faith, desecrating tradition. You've brought this city to ruin."

He didn't blink.

"No, no, that's an understandable mistake," he said, with a hint of sympathy. "But I think you're giving me far too much credit. You don't fear *me*. You fear your fellow man. Fear what they're capable of with the smallest push. How little it takes to steer them. That's what terrifies you, isn't it?"

His voice grew softer, almost mournful. "And it *should*. It's a shame some of them have taken to burning books… because truth and knowledge were their only salvation."

I shoved the blade higher, the steel kissing that pristine throat, his skin drawn so tight I thought it might split if he so much as swallowed. "Give me one good reason not to end you right here."

He didn't flinch. No tremble. Just those eyes, calm and clear, like a still pond beneath a full moon. "Name one good reason *to*," he said. "What would it solve, truly? Would it smother the fire in their hearts? Unteach the hate? Do you think they'd become forgiving, generous, and righteous as soon as their bellies were full?"

His unflinching, charming smile sickened me as he continued. "It will take *generations* of prosperity before those grudges die out. But me? I'm not the root. I'm the symptom. If you kill me, you make me a martyr. You confirm every whisper I've sown. You *become* the villain I've made you out to be. And you stain your so-called faith in blood. A tidy end. Yours, as well as mine."

My arms slackened. The weight of the sword suddenly too heavy to hold aloft. I let him go.

He was right. Of course he was. That was the worst part. One man could turn a city to violence with nothing but a smile and the right lie. But all my effort—every kindness, every sacrifice—had never stirred them to unity, only suspicion. It wasn't fair. But fairness had no voice here.

He didn't even dust himself off. Just turned, composed as ever, the picture of civility wrapped around something soulless. As he walked away, he glanced back just enough to say:

"People don't follow virtue. They follow certainty. You cannot deliver a message to those who do not wish to hear."

Then he was gone.

And I just stood there, blade in hand, as useless as a statue in a burning library.

The moon bowed low as I crossed the outskirts, its pallid light just enough to shape the path ahead. Rarek fell behind me in silence. No jeers, no bells, not even the sound of wind brushing the undamaged stone walls. Just stillness.

I walked with everything I owned strapped to my back and everything I was wrapped around my limbs. My body stitched with scripture, my mind weighed down by every line I'd ever believed, questioned, or rewritten. My burdens, holy and heretical.

Kirtana's verses silent against my arms. Eryndra's now stationed around my legs. Their distance stretched and followed me like a funeral procession.

And then there was the sword. Not the thing itself, but what it meant. What it asked of me. I'd once cast it aside, as one might cast away the sins of a past life. Just one more thing Eryndra resented me for. But I couldn't exactly remain a city guard if I planned to wander the countryside.

Now the blade hung against my hip like an old promise broken. I hadn't even used it. Not really. But already it had spoken louder than any scripture. Not one moment in my hand, and I was already threatening to silence another soul with it.

I didn't know what I was becoming. But I knew what I was leaving behind.

The burning remains of the crumbling chapel, holy stone defaced, lives discarded. The place where Selva drew her final breath, Eryndra gave up her belief, and Kirtana had hers cut from her throat. I left it to the flames and the silence that followed them.

I left behind the ghaf tree. That arrogant silhouette, its limbs stretched wide, leafed in defiance of the cold. Smothering the starlight, claiming victory over evil while the city burned beneath its branches.

I left behind a people so easily turned, so desperately hungry for hope, power, and blame that they'd devour their own neighbors just to feel full. Brainwashed into ravenous beasts, salivating at the first scent of otherness.

I left behind the false prophet from Talakit, cloaked in borrowed skin and golden tones, spinning the world with nothing more than a smile and a sermon, who twisted every sacred word into a sales pitch.

I left behind the dumpy librarian, hidden among his rolled maps and cowardice. Who knew the city was cracking and simply chose not to be underneath it when it fell.

And I left behind the blind, lost, spellbound child who needed my help but didn't want it. Who asked me not to hurt her and ran the moment I did. Who vanished into the walls and the shadows like a scar receding beneath fresh skin. I would never see her again.

I left all of it.

What I carried couldn't undo what I'd done.

But it was all I had.

Several days passed in silence. Not for lack of thought. I had plenty of that. Too much, in fact. Thought, and the kind of moral arithmetic that never solves cleanly. My mind kept returning to the same looped litany: the words I could have said, the ways I might have said them: softer, simpler, or not at all. All the tiny edits that might have made me legible to people determined not to understand me. My words, my actions, and my intentions were always received in the least charitable light. Even when no one was actively lying to further their own gains, they still mistranslated me into something threatening.

But even if they had understood, would it have mattered?

I kept wondering over how rarely words and actions seemed to line up in others. How those who claimed the faith with such fervor were the first to use its scripture as a cudgel, a barricade, or a mirror angled only to reflect others' sins. They could quote it fluently, scold with it proudly, invoke it piously—and yet none of them seemed bound by it. Not when it cost them. Not when it challenged them. The teachings were sacred, yes, until they were inconvenient. Then they became flexible. Symbolic. Allegorical. Optional.

I could still hear their voices. They wore the verses on their lips like a crest, paraded them at funerals and festivals, stitched them into banners and laws. But when it came time to actually live by them: to turn the cheek, to feed the hungry, to give up cloak and coin alike, they vanished. Gone like breath underwater. Scripture became something to hurl, not heed. They used it to punish, to exclude, to justify cruelty with the sickly smile of righteousness.

And I kept wondering: was a behavior wrong because it was harmful? Or only because it contradicted one line they'd chosen to remember from among many, divorced from context. If something good violates the letter of the text, do we reexamine the text? Of course not. We condemn the act. We smile piously and quote the rule. And then we do worse things in private.

I wasn't angry that they failed. I failed too, but I failed trying. Trying to uphold truth, honesty, and integrity, even when it cost me. Not redirect blame and avoid suspicion to keep my social life comfortable and my guilt quiet. What hurt more than anything, was that I was the only one still following the code they all claimed to believe in.

Shameful. Hypocritical.

And still they laid claim to the light.

I was so lost in the tangle of my own thoughts—wrestling ghosts, chasing old echoes—that the world around me blurred into distance. I didn't see the flicker of campfires behind me, scattered like fallen stars in my wake. Didn't hear the crunch of hooves on hardpan, the rhythm of pursuit. Didn't feel the burn of their eyes, hate smoldering where mercy should have been.

The crowd that had once cheered and wept beneath red and gold banners was hunting now. Not satisfied to exile me, intent on ensuring there was nothing left that could possibly return.

My feet came to the edge, and I stopped. Around me, the world changed. Behind: Rarek, kingdom of rot disguised as tradition, of zealots convinced they were righteous, of children abandoned by gods and men alike. And ahead: nothing. A blank scroll. The end of maps.

The grass beneath my soles thinned into cracked ochre. Blades that had fought to survive gave up their color, curling toward the dust. I stepped over the threshold, not knowing it would be the last time my feet ever beheld the green.

18 - The Last Witness

For days I wandered the dunes, sand battering my eyes, worming its way between my wrappings, scraping the last rough edges of my mood smooth. The storms here didn't scream with fury like those in the highlands. They whispered, hissed, wore me down grain by grain. The wind curled around me like a sneer, expressing the desert's disapproval, same as the mountain had. It dared me forward with the promise of assimilation.

But it didn't understand.

I was not a man. I would not wilt beneath the white glare of the sun, nor freeze in the breathless cold of the desert's dark. I would not beg for water that would never come. The land could strip me bare, and still I would walk. I would keep standing.

If the shrine was out here, somewhere beyond the realm of maps and men, then I would find it. No matter how hard the sand tried to make me one of its own.

Every few days, the horizon would spit up signs of life. Ramshackle outposts of canvas tents, crates lashed into half-walls, wagons long since stripped of their wheels and purpose. Bandits, exiles, perhaps worse. These were men who'd been severed from nation and name, who had learned to live in the lee of a whispering wasteland, beneath no flag but their own desperation. Survivors, certainly, but not the kind that prayed.

I never approached. Just watched from afar, their patchwork shelters like sores on the skin of the desert. Enough leather and board to break the wind, to keep the sun off their faces, to pretend that dying slower was a kind of safety. I kept my distance. Some predators don't need the promise of food to move them to action. They just need to be seen. Then strike to preserve their hiding places.

My feet dragged slower through the sand from the weight in my arms, and the shield on my back. My thoughts were worn smooth by the days of blinding silt. The wind had sanded them down to old grooves. No new revelations. No fresh reckonings. Only the ache of re-treading the same regrets. The same questions. None of them answered. But with precious nothing in the desert to offer distraction, they had just kept circling back around.

When I first saw it, I blinked, half-sure it was just the latest cruelty conjured by the heat. Some shimmering lie stitched together by exhaustion and the squint of wind-stung eyes. But the shape didn't shift like a mirage. Didn't waver. Just sat there, stubborn, waiting to be acknowledged. Angled stone, cut and quarried by human hands, jutting up from the dunes like the last knuckle of a buried fist. The wind had worked it over, softened its edges, scoured its carvings, but it couldn't undo what had been made.

It wasn't much larger than the chapel had been. The desert had claimed half of it already, but not all. A stairwell led down, nearly swallowed by drifting sand, and even as I brushed it aside with hands too tired to tremble, I could tell the partial burial wasn't entirely nature's doing. The stone face curved gently inward, hugging the dune like it was meant to nestle there. A shelter from the sun, from the cold.

From the eyes of men.

The moment I passed beneath the lintel and into the stairwell, the world changed. The air dropped heavy, thick like old wool soaked through. It muted the wind's howl, silenced the rasp of grit in my ears. My own footsteps dared not echo. There was stillness here. Not lifeless, not void. But… listening.

And I felt it. Deep in the lines of my wrappings, in the tautness of my shoulders. Purpose. Conviction buried here, as if this place had once held something sacred, and was waiting to do so again.

I walked the length of it slowly, one palm always on the wall, as though I might steady myself on the pieces of belief still etched there. The sand had done its slow, methodical work: softening edges, dulling clarity, leaving only fragments. Lines of scripture I half-knew, the openings of prayers whose endings escaped me. Familiar, yet fractured. Truth, once, but not whole anymore. And in the breaks between them, the shadows of doubt still lingered.

There were no pews. No benches, no cushions, no symbols of comfort. Just stone, unforgiving and absolute. The sand thinned here, swept aside by the breath of time or the ghosts of penitent feet.

This was not a church.

I'd seen this austerity before. In the temples near the mountain's pass, where the monks of old shaved their heads and bled their knees, believing pain could refine the soul like fire refines ore.

I passed through the final antechamber, and what a stunning site to behold.

The air faded here, like even the wind knew not to intrude. At the far end of the small room stood a shrine carved of unblemished marble that seemed untouched by time. A gauntlet—palm up, the fingers gently curled. Open and empty. Unarmed. The Right Hand of Tyr. Torm's symbol. A symbol of peace. Of giving.

Beneath it, lying in a lidless sarcophagus carved from the same stone, were the bones. Tattered vestments, but no ornaments. The flesh long since returned to dust. Even the shape had given way. I couldn't tell if they'd once been man or woman. And it didn't matter.

Because it was what lay with them that made my knees threaten to buckle.

Strips of linen, dozens, folded, tucked, and preserved. Their edges worn but the script still legible. Celestial, hand-penned, flawless. Just like mine. Just like Eryndra's. Just like Kirtana's. Scrolls, too, yellowed with age, brittle but their contents intact. Some verses I recognized. Others were variations: crossed-out lines, entire passages rewritten, refined. Some just abandoned halfway through.

Whoever they had been, they had written and rewritten until the truth sang like it was always meant to be there. Until it was ready to be sewn into something like me.

This was not a church, but it was not a grave either. It was a workshop. A labor of sacred obsession.

They'd died down here. Alone, by the looks of it. Elbow-deep in parchment. Surrounded not by family or followers, but by scraps of half-finished stanzas and bleeding ink lines. And they hadn't left so much as a note.

No name. No answers. No final thoughts spared for the creations that bore their voice and not their blood. Not even a single scrap addressed to us. Just the evidence of months, maybe years, of toiling in silence. Perfecting the script, refining the verses, until we were ready. Then nothing.

My creator, the one I had searched for, was here. And they were dust. And I would never know why.

Why write a man—nay, a *family*—into being, only to vanish before they could ask who they were meant to be?

Were we born in this place? If so, I remembered none of it. No gentle hand guiding mine. No voice to carry me into purpose. No parent to speak comfort, to show love, to walk beside us through the world they'd made us for. Just the wrappings. The hymns. The duty, baked into our bones like law.

They hadn't even come with us. Hadn't watched us grow. Just stayed behind and vanished. Perhaps they gave everything in the act of making us. Perhaps that was all they had to give. But it still left us alone. And it still hurt.

Why three? Each with their own voice, their own burden? Why abandon them? What were we for?

What was *I* for?

I dropped to my knees, the apathetic stone only adding to my pain. There was no answer in the silence. No warmth in the shrine's outstretched hand. Just the emptiness of a prayer unanswered because no one was left to hear it. Just a writer, long dead. And three voices left echoing without an audience.

I heard them before I saw them. Footsteps—six, maybe more—echoing through the vaulted halls. My heart clenched.

A voice rang out, mocking and determined: "We know you're in here, Ethereal! Time to finish what we started. Justice won't wait." A heavy crash followed. Shattered stone, perhaps a fallen statue.

I recognized that tone. One of the men who had shouted at me when I left Rarek with Luna. A survivor of the chapel raid.

I'd been followed. Their zealotry had brought them this far south, to the very doorstep of what might be the last shrine to Torm still standing. They wouldn't have tracked me here if they didn't intend to end me.

My grip tightened around the sword at my side. Cold purpose filled me. Righteous indignation burned beneath my skin. Principles be damned—no bastard would defile my birthplace, or my maker's rest. I'd already failed once; I wouldn't do it again.

I loosed Eryndra's petrified shield from my back, looping it over my arm and Kirtana's bindings. Their script stared back at me, just visible beneath the blood stains, and I read the words once more: *"Make a joyful noise unto the stars…"* Not tonight.

I settled into a guarded stance. Shield and sword at the ready, I whispered, "Stars… remember I was here." I rounded the corner into the main room, and waited for the first of them to step forward.

They were dead. All of them. Strewn across the stone, their blood mingling with the thin layer of sand that blanketed the chamber floor. And with my own. The air reeked of copper, sweat, and the acrid tang of spent rage.

I stood long enough to drop the shield, then the sword. They hit the floor in sequence—stone, then steel, then me. My knees buckled and my ribs crumpled in on themselves, and I collapsed onto my side, the breath shoved out of me. Every nerve screamed.

But I had to see it. One last time.

I rolled, barely conscious of the sharp lances of pain darting through my chest and thigh. I could feel warmth down my leg, spreading fast. The tile beneath me would remember in my stead. I clawed my way forward. Not far. Just through the archway. Just across the threshold where the sand had settled again like a blanket over the slain.

Every drag left a smear. The kind that wouldn't come out. The kind the wind couldn't lift.

The antechamber narrowed ahead, the stone rough and silent. No hymns here. No songs. Just me, groaning like a dying beast, dragging myself back to the womb I'd been drawn from. The shrine.

I reached it. Pulled myself over the lip of the room. Despite their constant screaming, I forced my legs to bear my weight as my slashed arms pulled me upwards and kept me steady. My blood darkened the hem of the linen strips that lined the inside of the casket, mixing with the dust and my maker's bones.

I pressed my hand to the stone base of the open palm, crimson forever staining the purity of the untouched marble.

I didn't speak. I didn't have the strength. I could offer no prayer, no apology, no thanks, no hope for the future.

My light flickered and faded, dimmer than it had ever been, but it held. I, however, did not. My strength ebbed with the last of my blood, fleeing my torn limbs in slow, traitorous trickles. My hand slipped free from Torm's affirming grasp, and I collapsed over the bones of my quiet maker, the empty eyes of their skull fixed on the ceiling, unwilling to accept this fate.

I was dying.

The stone beneath me felt colder than it should have. Or maybe I was just warmer, bleeding out my purpose. My limbs refused command. I tried to whisper a verse, anything, but my voice wouldn't rise. The scripture etched into me, the words I'd lived by, meant nothing if I couldn't carry them.

Would they vanish with me?

Was I the last? The final vessel? The closing line of a story no one else would ever read?

I had never known what happened to ethereals when they died. Would I dissolve into dust like my maker? Or vanish, unwritten? Would my light flicker once more, then fade forever? Was that all the will of a godless scribe could create: a temporary spark doomed to gutter out in some forgotten tomb?

Who would stand watch over this place when I was gone?

Who would remember?

I was still trying to find the answer when the darkness came for me. A quiet command I had no strength left to deny.

But my light, though faint, did not go out. It burned—a low, golden ember resting among the dust and linen, like the last candle in a stormed chapel. The last witness of a faith so pure, it breathed life into linen.

Epilogue - The Candle in the Dunes

They say a light still inhabits the desert.

Not the kind cast by flame or sun, but something older. Something that moves when the wind sleeps and the stars hold their breath. A gold-lit figure glimpsed at the edge of the horizon through dust-choked goggles.

Merchants whisper of *the Lantern Knight* whose glare burns through sandstorms. Pilgrims insist a *Hand of Mercy* walks the dunes, striking down jackals yet guiding lost children back to the trade road. Scholars prefer *The Last Witness*—a guardian forged from faith so old the pantheon that birthed it has no worshippers left to contest the tale.

Most dismiss it as heatstroke. A mirage. The brain misfiring under the weight of thirst and isolation. But those who have seen it, and lived, tell a different story.

They say the thing wears linen burned dark at the hem. That it moves without leaving footprints. That it never speaks. That it guards something buried, half-swallowed by time—a ruin of quarried stone, forgotten by the maps of men, nestled in the sand like a secret.

A temple.

None know what god it honors. The old reliefs are too weathered. The glyphs, too worn. But the wind refuses to settle there. And no scavenger who enters leaves. Sand gives way to half-buried steps, and when the intruders peer into the dark they glimpse a figure already waiting at the foot of the stair—a scarecrow of bleached linen, sword rusted with centuries of grit, shield made of bloodstained stone.

Then the wrappings split, the skull opens its mouth, and the light comes.

They say the creature is not a man, it merely resembles one. That it was something holy once—ethereal, made of scripture and song. But it has been sanded smooth by grief and time. Its name lost to the wind. Its face hidden behind sun-bleached bindings. A sentinel forged in sorrow and silence.

And yet, the desert does not take it.

Some say it stands guard over the bones of a forgotten psalm-maker. Others say it waits for the return of something it lost. A sister, perhaps. Or a daughter. Or a world that no longer has space for scripture and selflessness.

And sometimes, when the moon hangs low and the stars gather like an audience, it can be seen at the edge of the temple's weathered threshold, sword and shield at its side, linen flapping like torn banners in the wind.

Waiting. Warding.

Singing.

Some nights a voice still rises from the creature, pushing a wordless requiem unto the stars. Crude and untalented, but a joyful sound nonetheless.

One midsummer twilight, a raiding band finally reaches the inner hall. They have spears, oil, and bravado enough to laugh at ghost tales. The first torch lifts, and the circular room ignites, every syllable on the walls catching the flame and reflecting it until the raiders are painted in scripture.

They scratch their heads for a moment. No treasure. No coin. No artwork or tapestry.

The Watcher steps from behind the sarcophagus. Where its feet fall, the sand vitrifies into glass.

They thrust. The shield rises: the stone face of the chapel, pitted but unbroken. They slash.

The dull sword carves an arc, and shears the iron heads from their hafts.

Terror outruns greed; the survivors flee into night, leaving lanterns, oil, and one question none dare voice aloud: Why does it defend an empty tomb?

They never see the simple marble hand, palm up, forever asking and forever giving. They do not know that when the guardian retreats to that alcove it kneels—always the same spot, always the same silence.

They never see the tangle of linen unravel beneath the hand, fused to the bones of the scribe who wrote three lives into being. It no longer remembers who they were. Or who it was. Only that it cannot die while even a sliver of light remains to keep the darkness at bay.

So the legend grows, carried on trade winds and retold by hearthstones in quiet inns:
of a ruin no sand can bury,
of a story no time can kill,
and a lamp-eyed sentinel who will not yield the threshold—
because somewhere inside the husk and the linen and the borrowed bones,
a single truth endures, beating like a heart that has forgotten how to stop:

He still stands.

Author's Note

If you've made it to this point, thank you. This book, while wrapped in fantasy and fiction, is one of the most personal things I've ever written.

He Still Stands is a story about faith, but not in the religious sense. It's about faith in ideals. About holding onto integrity, goodness, honesty, and clarity in a world that seems to punish those things at every turn. It's about what happens when the just are left without justice. When compassion is treated as weakness. When staying true to yourself costs you everything… and you still can't let go.

Daelon is not just a character, he's a version of me. His sisters represent chapters of my life I've survived but can never fully shed. Their extreme, defeatist positions after hollowing keep recurring throughout my life, tempting me to make the easy decisions. I can't. I remember who they used to be, who ***I*** used to be, and I can't let that memory die. So, like Daelon, I picked up their wrappings, their scripture, their purpose and meaning, and incorporated them into myself as part of this new whole. I keep those past me's close, so I never forget.

As someone with autism, whose sense of right and wrong is rigid and absolute, I've lived with the confusion and frustration of being told I'm wrong. Wrong for holding onto ideals that others discard when they become inconvenient. I've been told to soften, to adapt, to quiet down, to fit in. But like Daelon, I couldn't. Aurelian Vale is the mask I've been told to wear—the charismatic, crowd-pleasing, adaptive personality that would make life easier… if only I could stomach becoming him. Murdering oneself, just to fit in, is a quiet, sinister, and tempting kind of evil.

Unlike the other characters, Luna is not one piece of a single person, she is a combination of several people from my life. People I have cared for, too deeply, too clumsily, too much, and too soon. People who didn't want to be offered a hand when they fell down, and certainly didn't want to be picked up. People who needed to believe in and rely on their *own* strength, not be coddled or emasculated by some would-be hero. Still, like Daelon, I was too concerned with "doing the right thing". I never considered that my good intentions and helpful actions could be perceived as the opposite. When met with stubbornness, I refused to take no for an answer. I dug in my heels and smothered the people I claimed to care about. I hurt them. If you are one of those people, please know that I am truly sorry.

This story is fiction. But the grief is real. The exhaustion is real. The isolation is real. So is the conviction. So is the hope—tattered, threadbare, but still there.

If anything in this book resonated with you, please know that you are not alone. And even if the world never thanks you for being the person you are:

Keep standing. — *Karl Smink*

www.ingramcontent.com/pod-product-compliance
Lightning Source LLC
LaVergne TN
LVHW090515110826
845146LV00003B/871

* 9 7 9 8 9 9 1 4 3 3 0 6 8 *